FINALLY A FAMILY

He was her first and only love. Claire MacInnes knew she'd encounter him again someday; even imagining what she'd say — so he wouldn't guess her secret. But now, that someday had come, Claire wasn't ready to face Daniel Hunter, or the feelings rushing back. How could she lie to the man she'd never forgotten — or to the daughter she'd struggled to raise alone? The daughter Daniel didn't know existed. Yet Claire wasn't ready to tell the truth yet, either . . .

MOYRA TARLING

FINALLY A FAMILY

Complete and Unabridged

LINFORD
Leicester

First published in
the United States of America in 1995

First Linford Edition
published 2012

British Library CIP Data

Tarling, Moyra.
    Finally a family. - -
    (Linford romance library)
    1. Love stories.
    2. Large type books.
    I. Title II. Series
    823.9′2–dc23

    ISBN 978–1–4448–1038–7

Published by
F. A. Thorpe (Publishing)
Anstey, Leicestershire

Set by Words & Graphics Ltd.
Anstey, Leicestershire
Printed and bound in Great Britain by
T. J. International Ltd., Padstow, Cornwall

This book is printed on acid-free paper

To my godmother,
Ma Simpson,
'Lang May Yer Lum Reek'

1

'Ten thousand dollars!' The deep resonant voice came from somewhere behind Claire MacInnes, shattering the silence and sending a murmur of surprise through the crowd gathered in the large ballroom of Vancouver's exclusive Shorefront Hotel for the antique auction held there each summer.

Claire spun around in her seat scanning the sea of faces in an attempt to locate the new bidder. She'd all but tasted victory as her bid of eight thousand had, until that moment, gone unchallenged. As she continued to search, her gaze came to rest on a tall, incredibly handsome, black-haired man wearing a dark suit, leaning nonchalantly against one of the pillars near the rear of the ballroom.

Shock ricocheted through her like tremors from an earthquake as she recognized Daniel Hunter's unforgettable features. The bidding paddle in her hand slid from nerveless fingers to the carpet at her feet.

Claire closed her eyes, willing the apparition away, but the action only served to bring to a deafening crescendo the roar of blood rushing in her ears, effectively drowning out everything and everyone around her.

She took several deep breaths in an attempt to regain control of senses gone disturbingly awry. She was dreaming. She had to be, she thought, as a wave of nausea swept over her, leaving her feeling weak. She shook her head in silent denial. Not Daniel! Not here! *Now now!*

' . . . Sold!' The auctioneer's pronouncement, followed by the sound of his gavel making contact with the wooden dais, resounded throughout the ballroom, slicing through Claire's chaotic thoughts.

'Sold?' Claire's voice was little more than a squeak as she opened her eyes and turned to stare in stunned disbelief at the auctioneer.

'And your number is . . . three hundred and twenty-one. Thank you,' the auctioneer acknowledged before flashing a smile at the new owner of the antique Steinway grand player piano.

'No! Please . . . wait!' Claire blurted out as she jumped up from her chair, astounded to discover that during those emotion-packed moments when she'd been lost in her own private world, the bidding had reached a conclusion. 'There's been a mistake,' she declared with more than a hint of desperation in her voice. 'I haven't finished bidding,' she hurried on, oblivious to the glares and frowning glances she was receiving from the people around her.

The auctioneer turned to peer disapprovingly at her over the rim of his glasses. 'I beg your pardon?' he inquired, annoyance simmering beneath his polite demeanor.

'I said . . . I wasn't finished bidding,'

she told him, her voice wavering slightly.

The man on the podium removed his glasses and studied her for a long moment, his expression grim. 'When I turned to you a moment ago, miss, you were shaking your head,' he told her. 'I naturally assumed you were no longer interested in the item, that you had dropped out of the bidding.'

'But I didn't . . . I wasn't . . . ' Claire stammered then stopped, aware with a growing embarrassment that practically everyone in the ballroom was staring at her. 'I'm sorry. Never mind,' she quickly apologized, wishing the floor would open up and swallow her.

Besides, she thought as she slowly sat down, there seemed little point in trying to explain to a roomful of strangers that she'd been shaking her head in stunned reaction to seeing Daniel Hunter, the man who'd haunted her dreams for the past eight years.

'Ladies and gentlemen. The next item in your catalog . . . '

As the auctioneer took command once more, Claire leaned forward to retrieve her bidding paddle, silently berating herself for her costly lapse. Ordinarily, Reginald Farmer, her boss, stepfather and owner of Farmer's Antique Market located in the interior of British Columbia, occupied the seat beside her and took charge of the bidding. But today he'd entrusted her with the job of acquiring the beautiful mahogany grand player piano on behalf of one of their most-valued customers.

After offering a few words of advice, and assuring her that bidding for the piano would be a valuable learning experience, Reginald had taken his leave, confident she would succeed. So confident in fact that he'd told her he would treat her to a celebratory lunch.

Claire had been equally as confident, especially when the dealer she'd been bidding against bowed out after her bid of eight thousand dollars. But the sudden bid from a source she hadn't been able to identify had caught her and everyone by surprise. And now she'd blown it!

Claire waited several more minutes before she stood up and headed for the nearest exit. As she wound her way through the crowd, she glanced toward the pillar where she'd spotted Daniel's tall majestic figure. It came as no surprise to her to see that there was no sign of the man whose appearance had affected her so profoundly. Perhaps she'd been dreaming after all, she thought wryly.

No. Daniel was here. Claire knew she hadn't been mistaken. Her luck had just run out.

Ever since she'd started working as Reginald Farmer's assistant in his antique store in Peachville, a small town in the Okanagan Valley of British Columbia, Claire had known that it was simply a matter of time before she and Daniel ran into each other.

After all, Daniel's family owned and operated Hunter Antiques, one of the largest antique dealerships in the eastern United States. As a buyer for the prestigious firm, Daniel traveled extensively to auctions and estate sales around the world in search of items for their many customers. He'd been in Europe on one of those buying trips when she'd met him eight years ago.

But it wasn't until Reginald suggested Claire accompany him on his regular buying trips that she had begun to prepare herself for the inevitability of meeting Daniel again.

She'd mentally played out countless scenarios of just how their first meeting would unfold, rehearsing numerous greetings in front of her bedroom mirror until she'd mastered a cool dismissive smile and a polite composed hand-shake.

She'd become reasonably confident that when she ran into him, she would remain calm and in complete control. But silently she admitted to herself that no matter how much she'd practiced, she still hadn't been quite prepared for the shock of seeing Daniel again.

Anger and annoyance and something less easy to define rippled through her at the memory of how she had reacted. She'd behaved exactly the same way she had eight years ago when she'd met him for the first time on a secluded beach near Camiore, a tiny picturesque Italian village on the shores of the Mediterranean.

The fact that Daniel was here in Vancouver was of no consequence, she told herself harshly. What mattered was that she'd lost the bid for the player piano, and in doing so, not only had she let Reginald down, but also the customer, a close friend of her step-father's, who'd instructed them to buy the item on his behalf.

Somehow she had to find out the identity of the winning bidder and then persuade him to let her buy it back.

The corridor was empty as Claire hurried along the carpeted floor to the desk where she had signed for and collected her own bidding paddle earlier that morning. The only clue she

8

had was the number on the bidding paddle. Her plan was straightforward. She'd simply ask the girl in charge to give her the name of the person to whom that bidding paddle had been issued.

However, to Claire's growing frustration, this proved to be easier said than done as she found herself at the end of a rather long lineup of auctiongoers. By the time she reached the desk, her request was met with a polite but firm refusal.

Much as she would have liked to argue, there seemed little point, especially in view of the fact that the people in the line behind her became rather vocal at expressing their growing impatience. With a sigh, Claire withdrew and retreated to the foyer of the hotel to think through her problem and chart another course of action.

Sinking down into one of the chairs near the row of telephones, she tried to work out just how she might go about discovering who had bought the rather rare antique player piano.

'Claire! Hi! I thought I might run into you today.'

Claire glanced up to see her friend Jane Styles. Jane was the assistant manager of the Shorefront Hotel and had grown up in North Vancouver, in the same neighborhood as Claire. They'd been friends throughout high school and had kept in touch over the years.

'Hello, Jane. How are you?' Claire responded.

'I'm great. But you look as if you've just lost your best friend,' Jane observed. 'Is everything all right?'

'No, not really,' Claire said with a rueful smile.

'What's wrong? Dani isn't ill, is she? Or your mother?' Jane asked, a hint of anxiety in her voice.

'No . . . no . . . it's nothing like that. Dani's just fine and so is my mother,' Claire quickly assured her friend.

'Did you bring Dani with you this time? She's out of school for the summer now, isn't she?' Jane asked.

Claire was silent for a long moment as she realized that, had Dani in fact been with her, as was quite often the case during school holidays, she would have glimpsed for the first time in her young life the man who was her father.

A shiver of alarm shimmied down Claire's spine, quickly followed by a feeling she could only describe as relief at the fact that her seven-year-old daughter had insisted on staying home in order not to miss the day-camp outing to the water-slide park in Kelowna.

'Claire, are you all right?' Jane asked. 'You look a little pale.'

'What? Oh, sorry. I'm fine.' Claire reined in her scattered thoughts and gave her friend her attention. 'No, Dani isn't with me. She opted for a trip to the water-slide park with her friends instead,' she said.

'I must admit that sounds like much more fun than coming to Vancouver to watch her mother at work,' Jane agreed.

'Well, if it's not Dani, why are you looking so glum?'

'I just came from the auction,' she said, motioning in the direction of the ballroom. 'I was bidding for a player piano, but I came away empty-handed,' she explained.

'Doesn't that happen fairly regularly in your line of work?' Jane asked.

'I suppose,' Claire conceded. 'But I thought I had it. I mean, it was mine — ' She broke off with a sigh of frustration.

'A player piano,' Jane said thoughtfully. 'I remember my grandparents having one of those, but that was a long time ago,' she added. 'What are the chances of locating another one?'

'Not good. They're rather hard to come by,' Claire replied. 'This one wasn't in perfect condition — the player action needed overhauling — but it was repairable.' She sighed again. 'I've been sitting here wondering what my chances are of finding out who bought it and persuading him to sell it to me.'

'Was it another dealer?' her friend asked.

Claire glanced up at Jane. 'I don't know. It's quite crowded in there, and I didn't see who bought it,' she explained. 'But if it was a dealer, I might be able to track him down,' she said, brightening a little.

'Well, if I hear anyone talking about player pianos, I'll let you know,' Jane promised.

'Thanks. I'd appreciate that,' Claire said.

'I'd better get back to work,' Jane said. 'How long are you in town?' she asked.

'We flew in yesterday and we're heading home tomorrow morning,' Claire answered, which was the reason for the urgency in tracking down the piano's new owner.

'It's too bad I'm working tonight,' Jane said. 'Maybe we can get together next time you're in town. Give my love to your mother and Dani,' she added.

'I will,' Claire said as her friend

turned and walked away. Claire glanced at her watch and grimaced. She'd arranged to meet her stepfather for lunch in order to celebrate the acquisition of the player piano. And she would have succeeded. She *should* have succeeded! But because of a brief emotional lapse, there would be no celebration.

Rising from the chair, Claire crossed the foyer and slowly made her way to the hotel's restaurant. As she waited for the maître d' to appear, she found her thoughts drifting back to the ballroom when she'd glimpsed Daniel's dark head and unforgettable features. She felt her pulse pick up speed at the memory, and not for the first time she wondered at her reaction to the man, especially when it had been eight years since she'd last set eyes on him.

Claire was reasonably confident that Daniel hadn't been aware of her presence in the ballroom and somehow she found that knowledge comforting. Forewarned was forearmed, and with the advantage of knowing he was here in Vancouver attending the auction, she could be on her guard from now on.

She and Reginald planned to fly back home in the morning, after they'd made arrangements to have all the items they'd purchased during Saturday's auction delivered to Reginald's antique store in downtown Peachville.

'Good afternoon, miss.' The maître d' smiled as he approached. 'A table for one?'

'Actually, I'm meeting someone. Mr. Reginald Farmer. Is he here yet?' she asked.

'Yes, he is, miss' came the prompt reply. 'If you'll come this way, please.'

As Claire wound her way between the tables she tried not to think about how her stepfather would react when she told him what had happened. She knew he'd be bitterly disappointed. She knew that if she'd been simply outbid for the piano he would have understood and accepted the loss. But the fact was she'd been in such a state of shock at seeing Daniel Hunter again and the treasure had simply been snatched out from under her nose.

'Here we are, miss,' the maître d' said as he stood aside to pull out the chair for her.

Claire felt her heart shudder to a halt when she found herself staring at the man she'd been thinking about, the man solely responsible for her present predicament.

'Claire, there you are,' Reginald said in greeting. 'I don't believe you know Daniel Hunter of Hunter Antiques in Boston. Daniel, this is Claire, my assistant and step-daughter.'

Daniel politely rose to his feet. 'Hello, Claire. How nice to see you again.' The deep rich timbre of his voice washed over Claire like a silky caress, spinning her back in time to that hot summer night on a deserted beach in Italy when he'd spoken her name over and over like a litany, while his mouth and hands had elicited a response she had gloried in.

'Hello, Daniel.' Her voice, she was pleased to note, betrayed none of the turmoil raging within her. Her body's reaction, however, seemed in direct contrast, numbed by the fact that the man who'd broken her heart so long ago, the man who'd touched her very soul, was gazing at her with nothing more than polite interest.

Misty gray eyes collided with hers holding them captive for what seemed an eternity. It was all Claire could do not to turn and run. What prevented her was the look of cool appraisal in the depths of Daniel's eyes.

He acted as though they were strangers meeting for the first time. And it was only because of the realization that any reaction on her part might be construed as some kind of a victory for Daniel, that she managed to suppress the urge to flee.

'You two know each other?' The comment came from Reginald who made no move to rise, but sat studying the twosome, a puzzled expression on his robust features.

'It's been a long time,' Claire said casually, as she lowered herself into the chair being held for her.

'How long has it been?' Daniel asked his voice steady, his eyes intent on hers as he settled once more into his seat across the table.

'Thank you,' Claire murmured to the maître d' as he shook out the white linen napkin and placed it in her lap, she was glad of the distraction, wondering frantically just how she was supposed to get through the next few minutes. 'It must be seven, or is it eight years?' she said at last, knowing full well it was almost eight years to the day. Meeting his gaze, she managed to conjure up one of the polite smiles she'd practiced to near perfection.

'Why, Claire, you never told me you knew Daniel. Where exactly did you two meet?' Reginald wanted to know, curiosity lacing his voice as he turned to Daniel.

'In Italy,' Daniel said evenly, but he

made no attempt to elaborate.

'Italy?' Reginald repeated after a lengthy pause. 'Oh, that would have been during the student tour you took through Europe at the end of your first year at Toronto University,' he said. 'That was the summer I met Claire's mother,' he went on, his voice softening at the mention of his wife. 'I remember Dorothy telling me that she hadn't wanted you to make that trip.' He glanced from Claire to Daniel and frowned before continuing. 'Wasn't it shortly after that you dropped out of school and came home?'

A frisson of alarm scurried across Claire's skin as Reginald unknowingly turned the conversation in a potentially dangerous direction.

Claire moistened lips that were dry and drew a calming breath before answering. 'Something like that,' she said noncommittally. 'In any case, that was all a long time ago. I'm sure Daniel isn't interested in my reasons for quitting university.' It took an immense effort to smile, but she succeeded. 'I hope we're not keeping you from anything or anyone, Daniel.' She turned to him, her smile still in place though her cheeks were beginning to ache from the effort. 'I'm sure you must have more important things to do . . . ' she added, hoping fervently that he would leave.

'Actually, no,' Daniel replied, a hint of challenge in his gray eyes.

'Then, please, you must join us for lunch,' Reginald invited magnanimously.

'Thank you, Reg. I'd love to' came the prompt reply. 'As long as Claire doesn't mind,' Daniel added, flashing her a dazzling smile.

Claire felt her breath catch in her throat at the latent sexuality behind the smile. During the past eight years she'd seen that smile a thousand times in her dreams, but she'd forgotten the intensity and power behind it, forgotten how easily Daniel could manage to evoke a response from somewhere deep inside her, a response that wreaked havoc with her senses, just as he was doing now.

'Why would I mind?' Claire said, trying to ignore the ripple of awareness dancing across her nerve endings. She reached for the water glass on the table, clutching its stem with both hands as if it were a lifeline, all the while fighting to control a body that was trembling as a barrage of memories threatened to overwhelm her.

Not now! Please, not now! she pleaded silently.

'Wonderful!' Reginald announced, picking up the menu in front of him. 'Let's order, shall we?' He beckoned to the waiter who'd been hovering nearby.

Claire was grateful for the momentary respite that afforded her the opportunity to regroup and repair the damage done to the wall she'd painstakingly built around her heart. Head bent, on the pretext of studying the menu, she silently chastised herself for reacting like an immature teenager just because Daniel had smiled at her.

She'd fought a hard battle for her independence and built a good life for herself and Dani, and she was determined that nothing — and no one — would disrupt their happy existence. Not even the father of her child.

Though her stomach was in knots, Claire ordered the chef's salad, doubting she would be able to swallow a mouthful, but knowing that if she said she wasn't hungry, Reginald would bombard her with questions concerning her health.

Bringing the glass of water to her lips, she stole a glance at Daniel's profile as he placed his order with the waiter. Silently she marveled at the fact that though she hadn't seen him in eight years there were few noticeable changes.

He was still the most devastatingly handsome man she'd ever known, with thick black hair, silky to the touch; finely chiseled features; a strong jawline courting only a hint of stubble; and black eyebrows arching over gray eyes that turned almost opaque with passion.

Claire's hand began to shake uncontrollably, sending droplets of water onto the white damask tablecloth. Instantly she dropped her gaze, admonishing herself for giving in to the urge to stare. She drew a steadying breath, willing herself not to panic. All she had to do for the next hour or so was to remain outwardly calm, keep the conversation away from herself and pray that Reginald wouldn't bring up the subject of his stepgranddaughter, the child he loved so dearly . . . Daniel's daughter.

'By the way, Claire,' Reginald said once the waiter had departed, 'I forgot to ask. Did you succeed in acquiring the Steinway for my good friend Alan?'

Claire's heart plummeted. Finding Daniel at the table with Reginald had made her forget about the loss of the piano. She swallowed convulsively, alert to the pending danger.

'I'm afraid not, Reg,' she said softly.

Reginald glanced across the table at

her, surprise and confusion evident in his blue eyes. 'What happened?'

'I was outbid,' she said, wishing indeed that had been the case.

'You mean the piano sold for more than twelve thousand dollars?' Reginald asked, obviously astonished.

'Ah . . . no. That is, I . . . ' She ground to a halt, wishing she had a better explanation to offer her step-father than that she'd mishandled the bidding.

'I'm not sure I understand.' Reginald eyed Claire, a frown clouding his features. 'I thought my instructions were very clear.'

'Your instructions were clear,' Claire answered as she fidgeted nervously with her napkin, all too aware of Daniel's presence and of the fact that he seemed interested in the conversation.

'I dropped my bidding paddle, and by the time I located it . . . ' Claire said, hating to admit her failure.

'The piano was sold,' Reginald supplied with a sigh, disappointment edging his tone. 'Do you know who the buyer was? Maybe you could make him a counter-offer,' he suggested.

Again Claire wished she could at least have told him the identity of the bidder. 'Unfortunately the ballroom was too crowded, and other than getting the bidding paddle number, I didn't see who bought it,' she said, her face growing hot with embarrassment.

'Perhaps I can be of help,' Daniel said effectively, capturing both Claire and Reginald's attention.

'You know who bought the piano?' Reginald asked.

'Yes,' said Daniel evenly.

'Who?' they asked in unison.

'I did,' Daniel announced, and at his words a feeling of alarm and a sense of foreboding washed over Claire.

2

Daniel Hunter watched with mounting interest the flash of surprise as well as the glint of fear that came and went in the depths of Claire's cornflower-blue eyes.

He was still recovering from the shock that had rippled through him in the ballroom half an hour ago when shortly after entering the room to see how the auction was progressing, he'd casually followed the auctioneer's gaze and located the person who'd been bidding on the Steinway player piano that was displayed on the stage.

At first he'd thought he was hallucinating. Claire, here? Impossible! But as he continued to glimpse her memorable features through the throng of fellow auctiongoers, he grew more certain with each passing minute that he was right.

With an action that was more reflex than conscious thought, he'd tossed in a bid for the player piano and before he'd had time to reconsider his impulsive move, he'd become the new owner.

Afterward, as he'd made his way from the ballroom, he'd asked several people if they knew the young woman who'd been bidding on the piano and been startled to discover that Claire worked for Reginald Farmer and was in fact his assistant.

He'd known Reginald for over ten years. As a fellow dealer in the antique business, their paths had crossed from time to time, though not in the past four years. This was mainly due to the fact that Daniel had handed over the job of attending the various auctions and sales throughout the country to his younger brother, Paul.

Spotting Reginald sitting alone in the restaurant had been an opportunity not to be missed, and after reacquainting himself with the older man and discovering that he was waiting for his assistant to join him, Daniel had sat down to await her arrival.

As he studied Claire across the table, he noted with silent appreciation the look of quiet maturity as well as an air of self-confidence emanating from her, characteristics that had been absent from the young girl he'd met on an isolated beach in Italy eight years ago.

Yet there had been something indefinable about her then, a youthfulness, a joie de vivre that he'd never forgotten. And if the truth be known, he'd never quite been able to banish the images of Claire from his mind, or for that matter, those incredibly exciting and wonderfully carefree days they'd spent together.

He felt a pang of regret that the chestnut-colored mane, which had once reached her shoulders, was styled into a more manageable length, framing her heart-shaped face and accentuating those classic cheekbones. Her body, too, had filled out nicely, with a fullness and subtle sexuality any man would notice and appreciate.

'Did you say *you* bought the piano?' Reginald's question cut through Daniel's musings, drawing his attention away from Claire, but not before he noticed that there was no ring on the third finger of her left hand.

'Yes,' Daniel confirmed. 'It's a rare piece and very collectible,' he continued, keeping his tone neutral, unwilling to divulge the real reason he'd bought the item. The player piano was indeed a collectible, and while he'd bid and won on a mere whim, he doubted he'd have any problem finding a buyer amid Hunter Antiques' many clients.

'Would you be willing to sell it to us?' Claire asked abruptly. 'We'll give you eleven thousand dollars. What do you say?'

'Claire!' Reginald glanced at her, surprise and more than a hint of reproach in his voice.

Claire felt her face grow warm as both men stared at her. She knew she was being impolite, but she couldn't seem to stop herself. It was bad enough that she'd lost her bid for the piano, but learning that Daniel was the owner was infinitely more upsetting.

'You must forgive Claire for her rather unbusinesslike approach,' her stepfather said apologetically. 'It's just that we've been on the lookout for a player piano for some time now and she's simply reacting out of disappointment. I don't mind telling you I'm rather disappointed myself,' he concluded.

'Are you interested in selling?' Claire repeated her question, ignoring the frowning glance Reginald cast her way.

Meeting Daniel again was having an adverse effect on her, Claire decided. Rudeness — deliberate or otherwise — was not something she generally indulged in, and her only excuse was that she had no wish to prolong this encounter, fearful that Daniel might decide to reminisce over old times, or worse still, start asking questions.

The past was dead and gone, and it was imperative that it stay that way.

'Before I answer, maybe you could tell me why the piano is so important,' said Daniel, and at his words a shiver of apprehension danced across Claire's nerve endings.

The waiter chose that moment to return to the table with their meals, and for the next few minutes no one spoke as he placed their respective lunch orders in front of them.

Claire was glad of the reprieve, using the time to reassess the situation. That Daniel had evaded her direct question for a second time left her with the impression that he had definite plans for the piano. Perhaps he'd purchased the item for a customer or collector, she reasoned, and if that was indeed the case then their chances of reacquiring it were decidedly slim.

But alternatively, Daniel Hunter was well-known for his business acumen, and it was entirely possible he was simply attempting to find out just how badly they wanted the piece in order to gauge how high a price they'd be willing to pay for it.

As Claire pondered the problem she reached across the table for the basket of rolls. Suddenly her fingers brushed Daniel's knuckles. At the contact, a jolt of electricity shot up her arm, making her jerk her hand back in alarm, almost knocking over her water glass.

Her gaze immediately flew to meet Daniel's in time to see an emotion she couldn't quite decipher flare briefly in the depths of his cool gray eyes, sending her heart stumbling against her rib cage in urgent response.

It was all she could do to drag her eyes from his as she fought to restore order to emotions spinning out of control. How could her body betray her this way? She hadn't seen the man in eight years, yet the briefest of touches had stirred her senses, awakening needs she'd long since learned to suppress and ignore.

It wasn't fair that even after all this

time Daniel should have such a devastating effect on her. She'd thought she'd securely locked away all her memories of the time they'd spent together, but every nerve in her body was quivering in response to his touch, waiting in heady anticipation to feel his arms around her once more.

Anger came to Claire's rescue, rippling through her like wildfire. She'd been eighteen years old and naive when she'd first met Daniel, and her tender young heart had been easily won over by the incredibly romantic setting and the devastatingly handsome man.

But he'd broken her heart with a callousness that had almost destroyed her. She'd managed, with the help of her mother, to work through the pain he'd inflicted, but the scars still remained, and she'd made a solemn vow never to allow any man close enough to hurt her again.

With great deliberation Claire drew a steadying breath, focusing her attention on the waiter as he refilled their water glasses, all the while willing her thundering heart to slow down.

'So, tell me, Reginald. Who is this Alan you wanted the Steinway for?' Daniel asked once the waiter had retreated.

'A customer. A very valued customer and a very close friend,' Reginald said. 'Alan Blakely has been collecting musical antiques for as long as I've known him, which is more than fifty years. He has one of the most varied collections of musical paraphernalia you're ever likely to see and almost everyone on the West Coast has heard of him or knows about his collection.'

'Alan Blakely! Great Scot! I thought he died,' Daniel said, obviously surprised.

'No, Alan is alive and well and living in our lovely little community of Peachville,' Reginald told him. 'He moved there, lock, stock, and barrel . . . when was that Claire?' he asked, looking across at her.

'Five years ago,' Claire supplied.

'Didn't he live somewhere in Washington State?' Daniel said.

'He did,' Reginald acknowledged. 'But he started coming to Peachville every summer, and when an old farm-house and outbuildings went on the market, he bought them,' he added, before popping a piece of barbecued salmon into his mouth.

'But surely Alan has a player piano in his collection,' Daniel said.

'Yes, that's true.' Claire supplied the answer. 'But a couple of years ago there was a fire in one of the buildings. That's where he stored some of his larger pieces and sadly he lost quite a few valuable items, including a Steinway player piano just like the one in the auction today.'

'What caused the fire? Didn't he have insurance?' Daniel asked.

'The building was old and the local fire chief said that faulty wiring caused the fire,' Reginald explained.

'Alan did have insurance,' Claire assured him. 'But some of the items he lost were quite simply impossible to replace. How often do you come across a coin-operated barrel organ in mint condition, or an upright Symponion with a disc storage cabinet as part of its base, or for that matter a Nickelodeon with a beautifully crafted set of flute pipes?'

Daniel met and held her gaze. 'Then tell me, if you wanted the piano so badly, why didn't you keep bidding?' he asked.

Claire felt her pulse kick into gear at the probing look in Daniel's eyes. The question caught her off guard and it was all she could do not to drop her gaze. But she wasn't about to confess that her reaction to seeing him again had been the reason she'd lost the bid.

'I told you I dropped my bidding paddle,' she said at last, knowing her excuse was lame and wishing she could relive those emotion-packed moments and change the end result. 'Now that you know we were buying the piano for

Alan, will you sell it to us?' she countered.

Daniel was silent for a long moment. For reasons he wasn't altogether sure of himself, he was reluctant to agree to her request. Though he knew Alan Blakely and sympathized with his loss, as he'd listened to Claire talk, he'd found his thoughts drifting to those moments when their hands had made contact across the table and Claire's startled response.

'From your silence I'd say you already have plans for the piano.' Claire's comment cut through Daniel's musings and there was no mistaking the hint of annoyance in her voice.

'Let's just say I'd like more time to think about it,' Daniel replied.

'We can't ask for more than that,' Reginald was quick to respond, possibly relieved that Daniel hadn't outrightly refused. 'Perhaps you'll let us know before we leave tomorrow,' he went on. 'When are you heading home to Boston?'

'I haven't made definite plans, yet,' Daniel said non-committally. 'I have some other business to attend to here on the West Coast,' he explained.

'You don't usually attend auctions anymore,' Reginald pointed out. 'Doesn't your brother, Paul, do most of the traveling and buying these days?'

'Yes,' Daniel confirmed. 'But he came down with a stomach flu yesterday, and I decided to come in his place.'

'How is your family, your wife? Did you bring her to Vancouver with you?' Reginald asked.

Claire felt her pulse skip a beat. She'd known Daniel was married; it was a fact she'd uncovered seven years ago, shortly after Danielle's birth.

She'd agonized for months over whether or not to let Daniel know about her pregnancy, finally deciding once Dani was born that as the father of her child, he had a right to know of his daughter's existence.

She'd succeeded in tracking Daniel

down to an exclusive suburb of Boston, only to arrive at his parents' home on the very afternoon of his wedding.

The taxi driver, who'd agreed to wait for her at the end of the long driveway, made no comment when she climbed back into the cab and told him to return to the airport.

Claire had spotted the actual wedding announcement in the newspaper the flight attendant handed her on the journey back to Vancouver. The item was in the society column and described Daniel Hunter's new bride, Kelly Albright, as a beautiful young socialite and the daughter of his father's business associate.

'Kelly and I have been divorced for two years.' Daniel's reply cut through Claire's reverie. His voice, devoid of emotion, sent a chill racing through her. She glanced across the table at him and saw a look of sorrow cloud the depths of his gray eyes, giving them a smoky effect.

'I'm sorry,' Reginald said quietly. 'I

know firsthand how painful divorce can be,' he went on. 'And children seem to take it harder than the adults. But you and Kelly didn't have children, did you?' he asked.

Though the question seemed innocent enough, the air was suddenly crackling with tension. Claire watched as the blood drained from Daniel's face, leaving in its wake a haunted expression that tugged oddly at her heartstrings.

He cleared his throat before replying. 'We did have a son,' Daniel said, his voice tightly controlled. 'Kevin died from Sudden Infant Death Syndrome when he was only two months old,' he concluded, with a slight but audible tremor.

Claire's breath caught in her throat at the pain and torment she could hear simmering beneath the surface. Hot tears stung her eyes and she quickly blinked them away, fighting the overwhelming urge to reach out and comfort him.

'My dear boy. I had no idea. Please forgive me. I'm so sorry,' Reginald said, obviously distressed, but before Claire could add her condolences, the waiter appeared at her side and began to remove the dishes from the table.

Daniel declined the offer of coffee and rose from his chair moments after the waiter finished pouring coffee for Claire and her stepfather.

'If you'll excuse me, I have a few calls to make,' Daniel said as he moved to stand next to Claire. 'Thank you for lunch,' he added extending his hand toward Reginald.

'My pleasure,' Reginald responded, accepting the outstretched hand.

'And if you change your mind about the piano, you will let us know, won't you?' Claire ventured, keeping her tone courteous and accompanying the question with one of her practiced smiles.

'Of course,' Daniel answered. 'It was nice to see you again, Claire,' he added, and before she had time to react, she suddenly found her hand enclosed in the warmth of his.

A quiver of sensation scurried up her arm. Claire lifted her gaze to meet his, and she glimpsed once more that look of anguish she'd seen in his eyes when he'd spoken of his son, an anguish he seemed determined to conceal.

Moments later he turned and walked toward the exit.

'How tragic,' Reginald commented, sadness etching his tone. 'Losing a child must be the most heart-wrenching experience for a parent,' he went on. 'Just the thought of something happening to Dani makes my blood run cold,' Reginald added with a shake of his head.

Claire swallowed the lump of emotion clogging her throat. 'Daniel's still hurting,' she said, managing with difficulty to keep her tone even, silently acknowledging that only someone who'd undergone a similar experience could totally understand the emotional effect of such a devastating loss.

Having a child of her own, Claire

could almost imagine the emotional wringer Daniel and his wife must have gone through. That he was still affected was obvious, and she knew she would never forget that agonized expression she'd seen in his eyes.

Feelings of guilt suddenly threatened to swamp her, and while her reaction was understandable in the circumstances, she couldn't comprehend why she felt such an overwhelming urge to go after him. The need to comfort him and perhaps ease a little of his emotional pain was strong, but Claire sensed that Daniel wouldn't welcome the intrusion, that he wanted to be alone.

Besides, it was really none of her business. She'd closed the door on that chapter of her life seven years ago when she'd decided not to disrupt his society wedding with an announcement that he was the father of her child.

While telling him about Dani now might alleviate some of his pain and dispel a portion of the guilt she was experiencing, it wouldn't bring back his son.

And even if she were to tell him, she had no way of gauging just how he would react to the news, she rationalized. She opted for silence, ignoring the tiny voice of her conscience telling her he still had a right to know about his daughter.

Claire sipped thoughtfully at her coffee, reminding herself that in less than twenty-four hours she would be on her way home to Peachville, where she could forget about Daniel Hunter and carry on with the rest of her life.

★　★　★

After lunch Claire returned to her room and spent an hour on the telephone making the necessary arrangements to rent a truck and driver to transport back to Peachville the items they'd purchased at the auction.

Reginald had returned to the ball-room to bid on a few items he'd

44

marked in the catalog. There were several battery-operated toys in good condition he hoped to acquire for a customer and collector in Kelowna, a box of silver teaspoons sporting a Scottish thistle on the handle for a friend of Claire's mother who loved anything with a thistle motif, and a Henry Boker mechanical corkscrew he'd told Claire might be of interest to Nathan Alexander, another valued customer and corkscrew collector from nearby Meadowvale.

As the afternoon wore on, Claire grew restless, but she firmly refused to acknowledge that she was staying in her room in order to avoid running into Daniel again. It wasn't that she was afraid of running into him again she told herself resolutely as she paced the carpeted room, it was just that . . . she was afraid of running into him again.

Eight years ago on a moonlit night on a secluded beach in Italy she'd fallen head over heels in love with him when she watched in breathless wonder as he'd walked out of the ocean, naked as the day he was born.

As the memory of that unforgettable moment washed over her, Claire felt her pulse quicken and her body quiver in instant response. He'd looked so utterly male, so incredibly vital and so stunningly attractive that she'd stood rooted to the spot, unable to take her eyes off him, until he came to a halt directly in front of her.

A need so powerful in its intensity suddenly clutched at her insides and she moaned softly in urgent denial as she fought to keep her memories at bay. She drew several ragged breaths and sat down on the bed, hugging herself tightly, desperately trying to hold on to her control . . .

A knock at the door shattered the silence. At first she could neither move nor speak, but a second knock effectively broke the spell and, collecting her scattered emotions, she crossed to the door and opened it.

'Reg told me where I could find you,'

Daniel said in a voice as chilly as a December breeze.

Claire shivered and took several involuntary steps back, startled by his sudden appearance, which served to compound her already-agitated state.

'Thank you. I will come in,' Daniel went on as he crossed the threshold and closed the door behind him. He leaned against it and gazed at her, his eyes glittering like diamonds, his expression grim.

Claire swallowed convulsively. 'Have you changed your mind about the piano?' she asked, suddenly recalling their conversation earlier.

'Forget the damned piano,' Daniel said abruptly. 'I have some questions that need answers.'

'Questions? Wha . . . what questions?' she managed to ask even as a feeling of dread began to spread through her.

Daniel took a step toward her, anger etched on his handsome features and evident in every line of his body. Claire felt the blood drain from her face at the look of contempt she could see in his eyes.

'I ran into Reg downstairs as we were leaving the auction and I invited him for a drink,' Daniel said icily. 'We had a rather nice chat,' he added, a hint of sarcasm in his tone.

At his words Claire's heart lurched painfully. She'd stayed in her room in the hope of avoiding Daniel, but she'd forgotten to consider Reginald in the overall equation. With a bravado she was far from feeling, she kept her eyes on Daniel, fighting the urge to flee, sensing with a strange inevitability that her safe little world was about to disintegrate.

'Reg told me you have a daughter and that her name is Dani. Is that right?' Daniel asked.

Claire's worse fears were instantly realized. 'That's right,' she managed to reply while her heart fluttered madly against her rib cage like a trapped bird.

'Reg also mentioned that Dani celebrated her seventh birthday on the first of May. Is that true?' The tone of his question chilled her to the bone.

Claire nodded, wishing for a frantic moment that she could somehow wave a magic wand and make Daniel disappear. From the angry glitter in his eyes and the questions he'd asked, it was obvious that after his chat with Reg he'd added two and two together and arrived at a stunning conclusion.

She watched as Daniel drew a deep breath before continuing. 'Then the question I'm about to ask shouldn't surprise you.' He paused briefly, his eyes staring relentlessly into hers almost as if he were trying to see inside her soul. 'Is Dani my daughter?'

The air was suddenly thick with tension, and it was all Claire could do to keep her gaze fixed on Daniel's as his piercing gray eyes demanded the truth. In her dreams she'd lived this moment countless times, but she'd always awakened with a start without ever having to supply an answer.

But this wasn't a dream! Daniel was

here towering over her like a tiger ready to pounce on his prey.

Claire moistened lips that were dry and opened her mouth to lie but the words died in her throat. All at once she knew that lying would solve nothing, that it was time to face the consequences of the choices she'd made when she'd learned she was pregnant, time to deal with the past and finally put it behind her.

Daniel might have fathered her daughter but Claire had been alone and frightened when she'd made the difficult decision to go through with the pregnancy and keep the child. Though Claire's life had been dramatically disrupted by Dani's arrival, she knew that if she had to do it again she wouldn't change a solitary thing.

'Yes, Dani is your daughter,' Claire said at last, surprised at how calm she felt and surprised, too, at the feeling of relief that washed over her now that Daniel knew the truth.

The silence that followed her words

was electrifying and Claire watched as a variety of emotions ranging from shock to wonder and finally anger, flitted across his handsome features.

As Claire's words of confirmation slowly sank in, Daniel felt as if he'd been hit by a speeding train. When he'd bumped into Reg downstairs and invited him for a drink, it had been relatively easy to turn the conversation to Claire.

But when Reg started talking about Claire's seven-year-old daughter, Dani, Daniel had suddenly found himself consumed with curiosity about the child. Reg, unmistakably proud of his stepgrandchild, had eagerly supplied answers to his questions, and with each answer Daniel's suspicions grew and intensified until he knew he had to confront Claire.

Now she'd calmly told him that the child was indeed his, that he had a daughter and it was all he could do to contain the rage rocketing through him.

'How could you! Why didn't you . . . ?

You selfish — ' he broke off and took several deep steadying breaths trying to calm his racing heart. 'How could you deny me the right to know I had a daughter? How could you be so callous, so unfeeling?' Daniel ground to a halt and, spinning away from Claire, he dragged a shaking hand through his hair.

Claire bit down on the inner softness of her mouth remembering clearly — as if it were yesterday — the anger and pain she'd felt eight years ago when he'd walked out of her life without a backward glance.

She didn't deserve his contempt. After all, he'd been the one who'd broken his promise . . . and her heart. He'd told her he'd meet up with her in Paris, but when the tour bus carrying the students she'd been traveling with arrived at their hotel five days later, he'd never appeared.

The clerk at the desk told her he had no record of Daniel Hunter, nor was there a message from him. She'd had no option but to believe that those magical days they'd spent together had meant nothing to him after all, that he'd simply used her then tossed her aside like a toy.

'I did try to tell you,' Claire said, her voice raspy with suppressed emotion.

Beneath the exquisitely cut Armani suit he wore, she saw the muscles across Daniel's back stiffen in reaction.

'What did you say?' he asked, swiveling to face her once more, his expression unreadable.

'I said, I did try to tell you about Dani,' she repeated and watched as his eyes darkened to a steely gray.

'When?' He bit out the word between clenched teeth, holding on, with obvious difficulty, to his temper.

'I brought Dani to Boston six weeks after she was born,' she explained, and had the satisfaction of seeing his mouth drop open in stunned disbelief.

'You're lying,' he quickly asserted.

Claire bristled at his tone, irked at his automatic assumption that she was lying. 'It was a beautiful day in the middle of June when I arrived at your parents' house in that classy suburb of Boston,' she told him matter-of-factly. 'But when I asked to see you, the manservant who answered the door politely informed me that you were preparing to be married that afternoon. Then he asked if I'd like to leave a message. I declined. With Dani in my arms I walked back down the driveway and into the taxi, telling the driver to take us back to the airport. We caught the next available flight back to Vancouver.'

'You came to Boston?' Daniel still sounded unconvinced, yet Claire glimpsed another emotion quickly controlled, flare briefly in the depths of his eyes.

'Yes, I came to Boston,' she confirmed. 'I brought your daughter with me. But when I learned that you were getting married — ' she broke off, surprised that the memory still had the power to hurt. 'What do you think I should have done?' she challenged. 'Should I have gone to the church and interrupted the ceremony, announcing to your family and friends and your wife-to-be that the baby in my arms was yours?'

Daniel was silent for a long moment and Claire watched as a look of skepticism came into his eyes.

'Why should I believe you?' he countered, his eyes glittering with an emotion she couldn't readily identify.

'I don't give a flying fig if you believe me or not,' Claire retorted, her patience stretched to the limit. 'Biologically you are Dani's father, but there's more to being a father than simple biology,' she told him scathingly.

'I still had a right to know . . . damn it! She's my daughter . . . my daughter.' He repeated the word, lingering over it as though he hadn't truly grasped the reality of it yet. 'What have you told her about me?' he asked, suddenly switching gears and going on the attack again. 'If she's seven, then she's bound to have asked questions about who her father is, or what happened to him. What lies have you told her?'

'How dare you!' Claire responded angrily, beginning to feel as if she were beating her head against a brick wall. Daniel seemed determined to believe the worse of her. 'Why do you assume I've told my daughter lies?' she asked.

'Haven't you?' Daniel asked defensively.

The telephone rang, startling them both and effectively defusing the tension reverberating between them. Claire spun away from Daniel and, crossing to the bedside table, picked up the receiver on the third ring.

'Hello!'

'Claire, glad I caught you,' said her stepfather. 'Daniel Hunter is looking for you. I had a drink with him in the bar and we had rather a nice chat. I told him you'd probably be in your room. Did he find you?' he asked.

'Yes. He's here right now,' Claire replied, glancing at the man standing in front of the window staring out across the city.

'Did he want to see you about the piano? Has he, by any chance, changed his mind about selling it?' Reginald asked.

'I don't know. We haven't discussed the piano,' Claire replied, wishing that had been the reason Daniel had sought her out.

'Oh . . . I thought . . . Well, never mind. I called to tell you that I bumped into Dennis Copeland in the lobby, and he's invited me over to his shop in Gastown to take a look at a couple of things he thought I might be interested in. Knowing Dennis, we'll probably end up having dinner together. Would you like to come along?' he asked.

'No thanks, Reg. You go ahead,' she replied, remembering all too well the last time she had accompanied Reginald to Dennis's shop. She'd spent the evening in a smoky bar listening to the two of them exchange countless stories about their army days together. 'Give Dennis my regards,' Claire added.

'Will do, my dear,' Reg responded. 'I

assume you've made the necessary arrangements regarding the rental truck.'

'Already taken care of,' Claire assured him.

'Good. I'll say good-night, then. I'll meet you downstairs at eight for breakfast,' he added.

'Breakfast at eight,' Claire confirmed. 'See you then,' she said before replacing the receiver.

'Would I be right in assuming that you're free for the evening?' Daniel asked as he turned to face her once more.

'It's rude to eavesdrop,' she told him.

'Not if it gives you an edge,' he answered smoothly. 'Besides, we haven't finished.'

'That's where you're wrong. I'd say we were quite finished.'

Daniel gazed at her in disbelief. 'You're a fool if you think I'm simply going to walk away after what you've just told me. Dani's my daughter, too.'

'First I'm a liar, now I'm a fool. You always had a way with words, Daniel,'

Claire said with a tired sigh.

'Damn it, Claire! We have to talk about this, about where we go from here,' Daniel said with more than a hint of exasperation in his voice. 'There's so much I want to ask, so much I need to know . . . '

Claire heard the pain and longing in his voice and desperately tried to harden her heart, but the knowledge that he'd already lost one child made it impossible. She didn't want to feel sorry for him, didn't want to feel anything for him, but her own feelings of guilt at having deprived Daniel of his daughter were already working against her.

Seven years ago, when she'd slipped away from Boston without giving him a say in just how his child would be raised, she had thought that her decision then was the only viable choice for everyone concerned.

But now she knew that no matter how much she might want to keep Daniel out of her and Dani's life, those days were over forever.

3

'Claire? Did you hear what I said?' Daniel's voice cut through Claire's distracted thoughts.

'No. Sorry . . . ' Claire felt her face grow warm under his frowning gaze.

'I asked you if you wanted to go somewhere and have dinner. If you'd rather, we can continue our conversation here and order from room service,' he suggested, taking a step toward her.

Going anywhere with Daniel was strictly out of the question, Claire told herself calmly, ignoring the shiver of sensation that chased down her spine as an image flashed into her mind of them sitting in a secluded corner of a dimly lit restaurant.

'I'm not hungry,' she announced, and at her words his expression darkened.

'You should be,' he countered. 'Considering you hardly ate a thing at lunch. Hmm . . . now I can understand why,' he added almost to himself. 'If you don't want anything to eat, that's fine. I'll order myself something and charge it to my room.'

Suddenly the thought of sitting in a restaurant with people around them seemed much less threatening than sitting here, alone with Daniel.

'I've changed my mind,' Claire said. 'It's a woman's prerogative, isn't it?' she added quickly when she saw Daniel's dark eyebrows rise in silent query.

'Fine. Let's go,' he said.

Claire hesitated for a moment. 'Why don't you go down to the restaurant and get us a table? I'll freshen up a little and meet you there,' she said evenly.

A slow smile curved at the corners of his sensuous mouth, causing Claire's heart to miss a beat and a familiar breathlessness to assail her lungs. But there was no amusement in his smoky gray eyes as he met her gaze.

'Why don't I wait for you here?' he suggested as he dropped into the chair by the table where Claire had been working earlier.

Claire bit back the protest that sprang to her lips. Then, with a nod of assent, she turned and headed for the bathroom, closing and locking the door behind her.

Though he hadn't actually said as much, his action had spoken volumes. He didn't trust her. With a guilty glance at her reflection, Claire acknowledged that she had entertained, for a few idiotic seconds, the thought of making her escape while he waited for her downstairs. But she'd quickly realized the futility of such an exercise. Sanity had prevailed. Besides, it would be so easy for Daniel to track her down.

Still, the fact that she should feel hurt by his obvious unwillingness to trust her surprised her. Turning on the tap, Claire let the cold water trickle over her wrists, all the while wondering just what Daniel planned to do now that he knew about Dani.

Dani! Claire twisted her hand and

looked at her wrist-watch. She'd promised as always to call home and talk to her daughter; it was a ritual they both enjoyed whenever Claire was away from home. A bright and inquisitive child, Dani liked to know what new item of interest would be gracing the store's window, and Claire liked to reassure herself that everything was fine by simply hearing her daughter's voice on the telephone.

Claire dried her hands, and reaching for her hairbrush, quickly ran it through her hair. Her call to Dani would have to wait, and in view of the dramatic turn of events Claire wasn't exactly sure what she should tell her daughter.

Daniel had been right when he'd assumed Dani had already asked questions about her father. At first Claire had been tempted to overromanticize the tale and tell her daughter that her father had died in an accident before he and Claire could be married.

But gazing into Dani's silvery gray eyes, eyes that reminded Claire each and every day of the man who'd stolen her heart so long ago, she found she couldn't lie, not to the one person who meant everything in the world to her.

Instead, each time Dani asked about her father, Claire had given a carefully edited version of the truth. But trying to explain to her highly intelligent child that her mother had been an immature eighteen-year-old who'd naively believed that a lasting relationship could be built on nothing more than a summer romance had been difficult indeed.

A shudder passed through Claire and she found herself blinking back the tears suddenly stinging her eyes. Silently she chided herself for allowing old memories to get the better of her.

She felt as if she'd been put through an emotional maelstrom and, glancing at her reflection in the mirror above the sink, she saw the fear and worry clouding her blue eyes. She wasn't sure just what she was afraid of. Daniel had no legal recourse regarding Danielle, but Claire couldn't help wondering just what his intentions were regarding his daughter.

Smoothing the skirt of her pink floral dress, Claire checked her reflection and reached for her lipstick and blusher in an attempt to add a splash of color to her pale features. Taking a deep breath, she unlocked the bathroom door and quietly rejoined Daniel.

He was still seated next to the table, elbows resting on his knees, hands clasped in front of him, his dark head bent as if in prayer, unaware that she had returned.

Claire halted in midstride and felt her pulse skip crazily as she let her gaze roam freely over him. Even in this somewhat relaxed position, his body exuded both an inherent power and an innate strength. She'd forgotten the impressive breadth of his shoulders and forgotten, too, the latent sexuality ostensibly hidden beneath the designer suit he wore.

She'd felt those muscles flex and

strain and ripple under her questing fingers, and delighted in the knowledge that she'd ignited within him such a fierce and primitive desire, a desire he'd aroused with equal intensity in her with nothing more than a smoldering look or a tender caress.

Daniel suddenly snapped to attention as if he'd sensed her presence, and as their glances collided, a frisson of need flashed through Claire, demolishing with ease the modicum of control she'd managed to garner while alone in the bathroom.

'Ready?' Daniel asked as he rose from the chair to his full height of six foot one.

Claire could only nod as she clamped down on emotions gone dangerously awry. She gathered up her clutch purse and room key, which she'd thrown on the bed earlier, and headed for the door.

The walk to the elevators was completed in silence and to her relief the elevator itself was almost full, allowing Claire several more minutes to repair the fresh set of cracks that had formed in the wall she'd constructed around her heart.

Stepping out into the lobby she walked abreast of Daniel toward the restaurant where they'd eaten lunch earlier. It was small consolation to note that judging by the speculative and interested glances Daniel received from one woman on the elevator and several more in the lobby, that she wasn't the only female around who found him attractive.

'It looks busy in there tonight,' Daniel commented as they drew near the crowd milling around the entrance of the restaurant. 'There's an Italian place a couple of blocks away. Let's try there instead,' he suggested.

Before Claire could respond, she felt his hand at her waist steering her through the crowd to the doors that led to a side street. A tingling heat spread through her at his touch, sending messages of alarm to her brain.

Once outside, Claire deliberately moved away from Daniel in order to break the contact, an action that earned her a sideways glance from the man walking beside her.

The late-afternoon temperature was pleasantly warm though slightly humid, not unusual for mid-July on the West Coast. Claire had to quicken her pace in order to keep up with his long strides. Glancing at his profile, she wished she knew what he was thinking, or more to the point, what he was planning.

Silently she acknowledged that she couldn't really blame him for his anger and outrage earlier. Looking at things from his point of view she recognized that it must have come as something of a shock to discover that he'd fathered a child and that the child was now seven years old.

Wanting to meet his daughter was a natural reaction, of course, but what then? Claire wondered, trying to keep in check the flutter of panic vibrating beneath the surface.

Claire felt sure that Dani would be absolutely thrilled to meet the man who was her father. In fact, Dani had been going through a particularly trying phase lately, determined one way or another to procure a father for herself and subsequently a husband for Claire. No doubt this stemmed from the fact that during the summer break she witnessed most of her friends' fathers becoming more involved in their children's lives, giving assistance to the coaches at softball or soccer games or simply spending quality time with their children.

Claire had become annoyed and at times embarrassed at Dani's obvious antics in trying to pair her up with someone. She considered every man that Claire had business dealings with or knew on a casual basis, who wasn't already married, as a potential candidate for the vacant post of father.

Dani's latest victim was Rick Robson, a charming young real-estate agent.

After much coaxing from both her mother and Dani, Claire had reluctantly accepted a dinner invitation from Rick only a month ago. To her surprise she'd actually enjoyed the evening out and since then he'd come to the shop numerous times on one pretext or another.

Whatever Rick's intentions, if in fact he had any, Claire was quite content to let things take their own course. 'Once bitten, twice shy' was the axiom she lived by, and even after eight years she was still unwilling to lay herself open to that kind of heartache again.

'Here we are,' Daniel said, effectively cutting through Claire's wayward thoughts, as he came to a halt outside a quaint brick-faced building with ornate iron grillwork across the windows and door.

Daniel held the narrow door open for her, and Claire, anxious to avoid brushing against him, carefully eased her way into the dimly lit restaurant.

As her eyes grew accustomed to the shadowy interior she glanced around at her surroundings, noticing immediately the intimacy of the place and noticing, too, how much it resembled the tiny restaurant she and Daniel had frequented during those four unforgettable days they'd spent together in the village of Camiore in Italy.

'Something wrong?' Daniel asked, his tone casual, his eyes intent on hers. 'If there is, we can go somewhere else.'

'No, this is fine,' Claire replied equally as casually, determined not to react, but wondering all the while if he'd been deliberate in his choice of restaurant.

Moments later, a dark-haired hostess with a welcoming smile appeared at their side and led them to a table for two by the window. Claire stared unseeing at the printed menu the woman handed her, her thoughts in turmoil as she tried to fathom why Daniel had chosen this particular place.

Surely he wasn't trying to rekindle their old relationship? At this thought her heart skidded to a halt then galloped on at breakneck speed.

Of course not! The idea was utterly preposterous! He'd broken her heart once, but she was damned if she was going to give him the chance to do it again.

She cast another quick glance around the small restaurant, noting this time with some relief that her initial impression no longer held true. Undoubtedly her memories were playing tricks on her. Slowly she began to relax a little, telling herself she was simply overreacting.

A waiter carrying a water jug filled the glasses on the table. 'Have you decided?' he asked, glancing first at Daniel, then Claire.

Claire nodded and proceeded to order cannelloni and a side salad, while Daniel in turn chose seafood fettuccine and a Caesar salad.

'Would you care for wine, sir?' the waiter asked.

'Claire?' Daniel said, his eyes looking with hers.

Tension shimmered in the air between them for several seconds. 'Yes, please,' she said at last. 'I'd like a glass of your house red,' said Claire, managing to keep her voice even, convinced without a shadow of a doubt that this time Daniel was indeed trying to elicit a response from her.

Each and every afternoon during those four days they'd spent together in Camiore, they'd walked into the village to share a meal at the local restaurant. They'd always declined the offer of wine, laughingly insisting that they didn't need wine, that they only needed each other.

Claire willed the memory away, urgently reminding herself that the past was over and done with, that they could never go back.

The waiter nodded and withdrew, and Daniel leaned forward, resting his elbows on the table. 'There's a couple of questions I need to ask,' he said.

'Fire away,' Claire replied with more confidence than she felt.

'How many people know that I'm Dani's father?'

'Only my mother,' Claire replied. 'I felt she deserved to know the truth.'

'And I didn't?' he countered with barely concealed anger, immediately putting her on the defensive.

'I came to Boston,' Claire pointed out.

'I only have your word for that,' Daniel retorted. 'Besides, you said that was after the baby was born,' he pointed out. 'Why didn't you contact me when you found out you were pregnant?'

Claire stared in stunned surprise at Daniel. He knew perfectly well why she hadn't. How could she contact him when she hadn't known where he lived?

'Daniel! I thought I recognized you.' The woman who'd suddenly appeared at their table was tall, blond and extremely beautiful.

'Patty!' Daniel smiled warmly at the new arrival. Pushing his chair back, he stood up and proceeded to hug the

74

blonde. 'How lovely to see you. Oh . . . forgive me. Patty, this is Claire MacInnes of Farmer's Antiques in the valley. She's Reginald's assistant,' he explained as he turned to Claire. 'Claire, this is Patty Buchanan. She owns an antique store in San Francisco.'

'It's nice to meet you,' Claire responded politely. 'I believe we've spoken on the telephone,' she went on, extending her hand, surprised at the sharp stab of jealousy she'd felt as she watched Daniel embrace the other woman.

'Of course. Claire!' Patty said with a brief smile and equally brief handshake. 'I was trying to locate an antique doll for a client, and you pointed me in the right direction.'

'Glad I could be of help,' Claire replied.

Patty nodded then turned to Daniel once more. 'When I talked to you last week, you said your brother, Paul, would be coming to the auction.

Darling, I'm disappointed you didn't let me know the change in your plans,' she scolded softly, her hand on Daniel's arm, her eyes gazing steadily into his.

'It was a last-minute thing,' Daniel said easily. 'Paul came down with a flu bug of some sort and I took his place,' he explained.

'Will you be free later?' Patty asked, obviously making the assumption that Daniel was involved in a business deal.

'Unfortunately, no,' Daniel said, regret in his voice.

Claire shifted uncomfortably in her chair, wishing she didn't feel like a fifth wheel. It was obvious there was some history between Daniel and the lovely Patty.

'But now that you're here on the West Coast, you do plan on paying me a visit in Frisco, don't you?' Patty asked in a breathless voice.

'Absolutely' came the laughing reply. 'But right now you'll have to excuse me. Claire and I have business to discuss.'

Patty threw Claire a speculative glance before turning back to smile at Daniel. That she'd been dismissed as a potential rival was blatantly obvious to Claire, but she was unprepared for the anger slowly taking hold, anger directed at both Daniel and the woman fawning over him.

For the first time Claire began to question her own wisdom in admitting so readily to Daniel that he was the father of her child. When he'd confronted her earlier, he'd caught her at a highly vulnerable moment. She'd been remembering a happier time, those warm wonderful days and nights they'd spent together in Italy. That, combined with her own guilty feelings, had undoubtedly tipped the balance, prompting her to confess the truth.

Though she wasn't altogether sure what Daniel's intentions were concerning his daughter, Claire suddenly realized with a pang that she hadn't even considered there might be another woman in Daniel's life, or just how that complication would affect Dani.

Fool! she admonished herself. Daniel was far too attractive and wealthy a man to be alone and unattached for long.

'Sorry about that,' Daniel said as he sat down. 'Now that I don't travel as much, I don't get to see Patty as often as I'd like.'

Fortunately the waiter chose that moment to arrive with their meals, forcing Claire to swallow the rude remark that had sprung to her lips.

'Enjoy,' the waiter said after he'd set the dishes in front of them.

'Thank you,' Daniel said. Picking up his fork, he glanced at Claire. 'Is anything wrong?' he asked.

'What could possibly be wrong?' Claire answered in a tone edged with frustration. 'While you were busy catching up with an old friend, I've been sitting here waiting for the other shoe to fall, wondering what you plan to do now that you know you have a daughter.' She stopped but only briefly.

'I'm beginning to think I should have lied to you about Dani because you haven't asked me one question about her. You haven't asked if she looks like you or even who she looks like. You haven't asked one single solitary question about your child. I should never have told you. I made a mistake, a big mistake — ' she broke off, fighting back tears, furious with herself for losing control.

'Now just a minute,' Daniel said, his expression grim, his voice edged with suppressed rage. 'If you think this is easy for me, you're wrong. I haven't asked about my daughter because I have so many questions I don't know where to begin.

'Damn it, woman. I'm still in shock, and on top of that I'm trying to keep a lid on my temper.' He drew a ragged breath. 'I'm angry, damned angry that you didn't contact me, that you kept this from me for so long. Angry that you deprived me of a chance to watch my daughter grow up. My son died before I had a chance to see him smile for the first time, or hear him laugh for the first time, or watch him take his first step. Do you have any idea what that does to a man?' He lowered his head for a moment and Claire watched his shoulders slowly rise and fall.

Lifting his head he met her gaze once more. 'My son is dead,' he said in a voice that was husky with emotion. 'And I'll always wonder if there wasn't something I could have done, something I should have done. And no matter how many so-called experts who told me that there wasn't a damn thing I could have done, I still have trouble truly believing it.

'Finding out I have a daughter is like being handed a miracle. And if you want to know the truth, I'm scared. Scared she won't like me, scared she'll think I abandoned her, scared I'll be a disappointment to her, scared that I'll wake up and discover this is all a dream.

'I don't expect you to understand

what she means to me already, but don't think for one minute that I don't care, because believe me, lady, I do . . . more than you will ever know.' He came to a halt, his eyes glittering with emotion, his body taut with tension. 'Let's get out of here. I've suddenly lost my appetite.' Daniel pushed his plate away and rose from the table.

Claire quickly followed suit just as the waiter hurried across to their table.

'Is everything all right, sir?' the waiter asked, but Daniel didn't respond.

Taking his wallet from his pocket he pulled out several bills and thrust them into the waiter's hands before striding toward the door.

Claire mumbled an apology to the startled waiter and hurried after Daniel. That she'd touched a raw nerve was evident, but he'd swiftly made her feel ashamed at her outburst and full of remorse.

She thought she understood, at least on some basic level, the depth of pain and torment he'd experienced at the loss of his son. But with a few revealing phrases he'd bared his soul, giving her a fleeting but gut-wrenching glimpse of the depths of the despair he'd had to deal with after the tragedy that had claimed his son's life.

Whatever pain she'd suffered as a result of his betrayal eight years ago was nothing compared to the misery and heartbreak he and his wife had experienced.

Claire called Daniel's name several times, but either he didn't hear her or simply chose not to answer. Not that she could blame him. She broke into a run in an effort to catch up with him, but he reached the hotel ahead of her and hurried inside.

The automatic doors swung wide and Claire ran through quickly, scanning the foyer for her quarry. She spotted him standing at the elevators.

'Daniel, please wait,' Claire pleaded as she put her hand on his suit sleeve as he took a step toward an open elevator.

He came to a halt and, turning, met

her gaze, his expression guarded.

'I'm sorry,' she said softly, but her apology brought no visible change to his strained features. Claire tried again. 'Please, can we talk?' Beneath her fingers she felt some of the tension slowly ebb away. 'I guess I'm feeling defensive as well as a little protective,' she said. 'This isn't exactly a walk in the park for me, either, you know.'

Daniel nodded and gently ushered her away from the elevators to the alcove at the right of the front desk.

'This isn't easy for either of us,' he said evenly. 'But hear this, Claire. I do want to know everything there is to know about my daughter. I want to meet her and get to know her, but I'm not totally insensitive. And I certainly don't intend to barge into her life like a bull in a china shop and announce who I am.'

'I know,' Claire said, knowing she'd overreacted. 'Listen, you said you have some business in town. When I go home tomorrow, I'll suggest to Dani that we come to Vancouver for a few days of shopping. She loves to shop. We could run into you here at the hotel . . . '

'Claire! Claire!'

Claire turned to see her friend Jane bearing down on them, a look of concern on her face.

'What's wrong?' Claire asked, sensing an urgency in Jane's demeanor.

'I called your room but you weren't there,' Jane said. 'I've been trying to find you. You had a call from the hospital in Peachville . . . '

'The hospital?' Claire repeated, fighting down the panic suddenly clutching at her insides. 'Dear God! What happened? Is it Dani? Is she all right?'

4

'Dani's fine,' Jane was quick to reply. 'It's your mother. She's been taken to the hospital,' her friend explained.

'My mother?' Claire said, and felt herself sway as conflicting feelings of relief and concern warred within her.

A strong arm encircled her waist, holding her steady, and she flashed Daniel a grateful glance, having forgotten momentarily he was there.

'What happened? Is she all right?' she asked breathlessly, controlling with difficulty the fear racing through her, mingled with other sensations that were equally as disconcerting.

'He didn't say,' Jane answered. 'You weren't in your room and so the caller asked to talk to a senior staff member. The call was put through to my office,' she explained. 'He told me your mother had been brought in by ambulance and that you or your stepfather should call Dr. McGregor at the hospital in Peachville as soon as possible.'

'Oh, dear. Reginald. I must find him,' Claire said, anxiety creeping into her voice now.

'Did he tell you where he was going?' Daniel asked calmly, his arm still around her waist.

'He said he was having dinner with Dennis Copeland. Dennis owns a shop in Gastown,' she told him, trying with difficulty to ignore the knot of heat where his hand rested.

'The Treasure Trove,' Daniel supplied.

'That's right . . . ' Claire said.

'I've known Dennis for years,' he informed her. 'Look, why don't you call the hospital and find out how your mother is and I'll call Dennis and see if Reginald is still there.'

'Would you?' Claire asked, turning to face him, grateful for his support and glad of his presence.

'Of course,' he responded and,

looking into his eyes, Claire felt strangely reassured.

'You can use the phone in my office, Claire,' Jane said.

'Right. Thank you,' Claire said, distracted momentarily by the warmth and concern she'd seen in the depths of Daniel's gray eyes.

As she followed Jane toward her office, which was directly across from the registration desk, Claire's thoughts instantly turned to her mother and Dani. A shiver of apprehension rippled down her spine. What could have happened?

'Would you like me to stay?' Jane asked.

'No . . . that's all right,' Claire replied as she reached for the telephone.

As Jane closed the office door behind her, Claire dialed the operator and asked to be put through to the hospital in Peachville. It took several minutes before the hospital switchboard finally located the doctor.

'Dr. McGregor . . . Bruce? This is

Claire MacInnes. I'm calling from Vancouver. It's about my mother, Dorothy Farmer. Is she all right? I was told you'd called,' she said, her voice wavering slightly, her hands clenched tightly around the receiver.

'Claire! Hello!' the doctor greeted her. 'First, let me put your fears to rest and say that your mother is resting comfortably.'

'What happened? Was there an accident? Is Dani hurt?' Claire stumbled over the questions, fearful of the answers.

'Dani's just fine,' Bruce replied. 'No, it wasn't an accident. We're fairly sure your mother suffered a mild heart attack.'

'A heart attack!'

'A minor one. She's fine. I assure you,' Bruce repeated. 'But I want to keep her in overnight for observation and possibly for a few more days,' he told her calmly.

At his reassuring tone Claire's panic began to ebb. 'Where's Dani? Is she there?' she asked, her concern now for her daughter.

'Yes, she's here at the hospital. There's a nurse keeping an eye on her at the moment,' he told her. 'She's fine, too. Got a bit of a fright, but she was a real trooper and handled herself very well. You should be proud of her.'

The thought of Dani coping on her own was more than Claire could bear. 'Listen, Bruce. I'm going to try and get Reginald and I on a flight home tonight,' Claire said. 'Unfortunately, Reginald isn't here at the moment but as soon as he gets back, we'll head to the airport.'

'Good,' Bruce said. 'We'll keep Dani here until you arrive. But if you aren't able to get a flight tonight, let me know and I'll make arrangements for her to spend the night here.'

'But they are both all right?' Claire asked again, wishing she was there and able to see for herself.

'Absolutely,' Bruce confirmed. 'Try not to worry, Claire. And if all goes well, I'll see you in a few hours.'

'Yes . . . thanks, Bruce. And please

give my mother and Dani my love,' she said before hanging up.

At the sound of a knock, Claire turned to find Daniel standing in the doorway.

'Did you find Reginald?' she asked.

'I talked to Dennis. He said Reginald had already left. He should be getting back here very soon,' Daniel said. 'How's your mother?' he asked as he came farther into the room, letting the door close behind him.

'She had a heart attack,' Claire said. 'But only a mild one, thank heavens.'

'I'm so sorry, Claire.' Daniel came to a halt in front of her. 'Is she all right?' he asked softly.

'She's resting comfortably,' Claire replied, her voice husky with emotion. She lowered her head, a numbness washing over her as the realization of what had happened began to sink in.

'Claire, she'll be all right.' Daniel's voice was full of compassion, and she felt his hands gently grasp her upper arms, holding her steady.

Slowly she lifted her head to meet his gaze. The look of concern she could see in his eyes was her undoing and a tear spilled over to trickle down her cheek, followed by another and another.

'Hey, don't cry,' Daniel said, his voice tender, as he pulled her against his solid frame.

Claire closed her eyes and simply gave herself up to the need to be comforted. She drew a steadying breath and with it came the scent of earth and trees, mingling with another more erotic scent that was entirely too male, a scent that stirred her senses and set her heart beating a shade too fast.

Jolted by her reaction, she quickly pulled away, moving out of his arms to hastily wipe the wetness from her face. 'I'm sorry . . . ' she mumbled, annoyed with herself for her show of weakness and annoyed, too, at her response to his nearness.

'Don't be,' Daniel replied easily. 'You've had a shock. It's only natural,' he went on. 'Come on . . . We'd better see if Reginald's back yet,' he suggested.

He held the door open and they emerged from the office just in time to see Reginald crossing the expansive lobby on his way to the bank of elevators.

'Reginald!' Claire's call brought her stepfather to a halt.

'Hello, you two.' Reginald greeted them with a smile that faded as Claire and Daniel approached. 'Something's wrong. What is it?' he asked anxiously.

'It's Mom — she's been taken to hospital,' Claire said. 'She's all right,' she added, taking her stepfather's hand in an attempt to reassure him.

'What happened?' Reginald asked, his face pale.

'I called the hospital and talked to Dr. McGregor,' Claire said evenly. 'He said Mom suffered a mild heart attack, but she's resting comfortably.' At her words Reginald squeezed her hand in his.

'You're sure she's all right?' Reginald

asked and Claire saw the fear in her stepfather's eyes.

'Yes, I'm sure,' she repeated. 'Look, this isn't the place to talk,' she went on. 'Let's go upstairs and you can call the hospital and talk to the doctor yourself, while I try to get us on a flight back home tonight.'

'Good idea,' Reginald said, though he still seemed in somewhat of a daze as he allowed Claire and Daniel to usher him into a waiting elevator. Their rooms on the tenth floor were adjoining and Claire used her key to gain entry.

'Do you want to call the doctor?' Claire asked once they were all inside.

'Yes . . . yes, I do,' Reginald replied. 'What about Dani? Was there an accident? Is she all right?' Reginald wanted to know.

'They weren't involved in an accident. Dani's fine,' Claire quickly assured him. 'Call the operator first. It's faster,' she went on.

'Right,' Reginald said, but he didn't move, obviously still dealing with the shock he'd received.

'Why don't I make the call for you?' Daniel suggested as he followed Reginald into the adjoining room.

Claire reached for her telephone and with the help of the information booklet the hotel supplied, she placed a call to the airline and asked if they could get on an earlier flight.

But five very frustrating minutes later Claire replaced the receiver. There were no flights to Peachville tonight. The only flight was the one they were already booked on, leaving late the following morning.

'Did you talk to Dr. McGregor?' Claire asked as she crossed the threshold into Reginald's room.

'Yes, but he didn't have anything new to tell me,' Reginald answered. 'Did you get us on a flight?' he asked.

'I'm afraid not,' Claire replied, disappointment echoing in her voice. 'There's nothing until our scheduled flight tomorrow,' she said.

'Surely there must be some way of

getting home tonight,' Reginald said agitatedly. 'We can't just sit around here. Your mother needs me . . . '

'I might be able to arrange transportation for you.' Daniel's words captured both Claire and Reginald's attention. They turned to look at him.

'We'd be eternally grateful,' Reginald said. 'But how?'

'If you'll excuse me for a few minutes, I'll go to my room and hunt up a few telephone numbers and then make a few calls . . . ' he told them.

'By all means,' Reginald said. 'Thank you, Daniel. It's very kind of you.'

'Not at all.' Daniel waved away his thanks. 'I'll be right back,' he said, and with a brief smile he was gone.

When the door closed behind Daniel, Claire turned to her stepfather. 'I doubt Daniel will have any luck, either,' she said, not wanting Reginald to get his hopes up too high. 'I'd better call Dr. McGregor and ask him to keep Dani at the hospital until we can get there tomorrow.'

'Let's wait,' Reginald said. 'Another ten minutes isn't going to matter one way or the other. And who knows — Daniel might just succeed,' he added optimistically. 'I think I'll pack, just in case.'

Claire said nothing as she returned to her own room. Silently she said a prayer that Daniel would indeed succeed. As she gathered her clothes together, her thoughts drifted back to those moments in Jane's office when she'd felt the warmth and comfort of his arms. A shiver of awareness shimmied down her spine at the memory. It had been a long time since she'd known the sweet solace of a man's arms.

Throughout the ordeal he'd been like a rock, steadfast and solid, giving support without ever being asked. His own anger at her earlier had given way to concern on learning the gravity of the situation. He was certainly someone worth having around in a crisis, Claire thought.

Resolutely she pulled her thoughts

away from Daniel and, entering the bathroom, collected her toiletries. Tucking the last of her things into the suitcase, she zippered it shut. All that mattered at the moment was getting home to her mother and Dani, and if Daniel could accomplish that feat they'd be deeply in his debt.

Twenty minutes later Reginald answered a knock on his door. 'Daniel! Come on in,' he invited.

At the sound of her stepfather's voice, Claire hurried to the adjoining bedroom.

'If you're ready, I'll take you to the airport now,' Daniel told them, and Claire had to curb the impulse to throw herself into his arms.

'That's wonderful, isn't it, Claire?' Reginald turned to smile at her. 'I don't know how you did it, son, but we thank you,' he added as he extended his hand to the younger man.

'Glad I could help,' Daniel said sincerely.

Taking advantage of the hotel's quick

check-out system, Claire and Reginald, luggage in hand, were soon ready to leave.

'How did you do it?' Claire asked five minutes later as they followed Daniel out to his rental car.

'Does it matter?' Daniel replied easily as he held the front passenger door open for her.

The drive through the downtown area was completed in silence. But when Daniel ignored the signs indicating the route to Vancouver International Airport, Claire threw him a questioning glance.

'You missed the turn,' she said.

'I know,' he answered evenly. 'It's a private jet. We leave from one of the smaller airfields,' he told her before she could ask.

'You hired a private jet?' Claire said incredulously.

'Not exactly,' said Daniel.

'What do you mean, not exactly?' she countered, as her heart gave one quick unsteady leap.

'The twin-engined jet belongs to me,' he told her, matter-of-factly. 'I flew it here myself. I have a pilot's license. Actually, I'll be your pilot tonight.' He flashed her a smile before adding, 'I hope that isn't a problem.'

'You're a man with hidden talents, Daniel,' said Reginald from the back seat. 'Are you sure this isn't too much of an inconvenience for you?'

'Not at all,' Daniel assured him. 'Besides, all I did was call ahead and have the jet fueled up. Then I consulted my charts and drew up a flight plan,' he explained.

Claire was silent, still trying to recover from the shock of learning Daniel would be their pilot. Much as she might want to object, their goal was to get back to Peachville as quickly as possible. If Daniel hadn't been around, she and Reginald would have had no choice but to stay in Vancouver and fly out as scheduled in the morning, spending a sleepless night worrying. At least this way they'd be home in a few hours.

'How small a plane is it?' Reginald asked from the back seat.

'Jet . . . ' he corrected. 'And it can carry eight passengers,' Daniel replied.

Half an hour later Claire climbed the steps of the twin-engined jet. She chose a seat behind and to the right of the pilot while Reginald at Daniel's invitation occupied the seat generally reserved for a co-pilot. After strapping himself in to the pilot's seat, Daniel immediately began a routine preflight check.

Outside, it was still daylight, long summer evenings stretching the days to their fullest as the sun lazily made its way toward the horizon. Claire watched with interest as Daniel, his features creased in concentration, went through the mandatory ritual.

As the engines came to life, she continued to watch, fascinated by the array of dials in front of him, and the way his hands moved with a sureness that came from inner confidence. Claire felt herself slowly relaxing.

The takeoff was as smooth, if not smoother, than any Claire had ever experienced. No one spoke as Daniel took the plane higher and higher. The city fell away beneath them, finally disappearing altogether as they soared above the clouds.

Claire once again turned to look at Daniel and her heart skipped a beat as she drank in his handsome profile, long ago imprinted in her mind. Eight years ago, when he'd walked naked out of the surf and into her life, his classic features had instantly reminded her of the pictures of Greek gods she'd seen in her history books at school.

Her pulse took another leap when her gaze fell to his hands, his long fingers holding the controls with practiced ease. All at once, the memory of Daniel's hands skimming over her body, leaving a trail of fire in their wake, washed over her, awakening needs she'd long since forgotten.

Closing her eyes, Claire struggled to stop the sudden onrush of erotic images threatening to overwhelm her. With fierce determination she pushed the memories back into the dark recesses of her mind.

Overloaded hormones, that's all it was, she told herself, resolutely refusing to acknowledge that Daniel's reappearance in her life was creating havoc with her senses.

'When did you learn to fly?' Reginald's question effectively distracted her, and for a while Claire listened with interest to Daniel tell of his first flying lesson, six years ago. It wasn't long, however, before the sound of his voice and the rhythmic noise of the jet's engines lulled her into a fitful sleep.

Forty-five minutes later a change in the engine noise awakened her. It didn't take her long, even in her groggy state to realize that Daniel had begun the plane's descent. Outside, the sky was darkening, and looking down, Claire saw an array of twinkling lights that was Peachville.

'Your father's retired now, isn't he?'

she heard Reginald ask and waited for Daniel to respond.

'For some time now,' Daniel confirmed, reaching out to flip a switch in front of him.

'I've been thinking about retiring myself,' Reginald said. 'I'm sixty-eight years old. I think it's time. Don't you?'

'You've been in the antique business a long time, Reg,' Daniel said, respect in his tone.

'Too long,' Reginald said with a sigh. 'But you know, these past eight years, since Dorothy came into my life . . . well . . . they've been some of the best years of my life.'

Claire smiled in the darkness, hearing the love and sincerity in her stepfather's voice.

'You're a lucky man,' Daniel said with a hint of sadness that tugged strangely at Claire's heart.

'I am indeed,' came the reply. 'And that's the reason I think perhaps I should be devoting more time to her . . . to us,' he corrected. 'Who knows how many years we have left together.'

Claire felt tears prick her eyes as she listened to Reginald. His marriage to her mother, the Christmas before Dani was born, had been a small private affair but Claire couldn't recall ever seeing a happier pair.

They'd met the summer Claire had toured Europe. Dorothy, who'd grown up in Peachville, had been visiting her old school friend, Joyce Alexander, in nearby Meadowvale when she'd been introduced to Reginald at a neighborhood barbecue. As her mother liked to tell it, it had been love at first sight.

'We'll be landing in approximately five minutes.' Daniel's announcement cut through Claire's musings. After checking that her seat belt was still fastened, she gazed with fondness at the town below, a place that had been her home since before Dani was born.

When Reginald married her mother, he'd generously extended Claire a warm welcome as part of his extended family, and on her return from her disastrous trip to Boston with baby Dani, had immediately offered her a job in his store as his assistant, brushing aside her protests, simply saying he needed someone to look after the business while he ventured to sales and auctions.

Determined that he should never feel cause to regret his impulsive and generous gesture, Claire had devoted herself to learning the business inside out, and to her surprise and pleasure had loved every minute of it.

When the wheels of the twin-engined jet touched down on the tarmac a few minutes later, Claire released the breath she hadn't known she'd been holding.

'Are you planning to fly back to Vancouver tonight?' Reginald asked as the plane taxied toward the buildings at the end of the short runway that was part of the small airfield situated on the outskirts of Peachville.

'Well — ' Daniel began.

'We'd be more than happy to put you

up for the night,' Reginald quickly cut in. 'After all the trouble you've gone to on our behalf, it's the least we can do. Don't you agree, Claire?' he added, twisting in his seat to look at her.

'Yes, of course,' she replied after the briefest of hesitations, all the while aware of Daniel's gaze on her. Had he planned on staying? she wondered. A few hours ago he'd learned he had a daughter, right here in Peachville. Perhaps that had been at the back of his mind when he'd offered to fly them home. But in all honesty she couldn't blame him for taking advantage of the opportunity that had presented itself. And she couldn't in all conscience send him away without at least seeing Dani.

'We have to make a detour to the hospital first, of course,' Reginald continued as one by one they descended the steps of the jet.

'No problem,' Daniel said as they crossed the tarmac to the buildings.

After loading the luggage into the

taxi, the driver took them through town to the hospital. As they pulled up outside the emergency area, Claire's thoughts turned to her mother and Dani and the drama that had unfolded for them.

Her mother had always enjoyed good health, and now at the age of seventy prided herself in keeping active. Since Dani's arrival on the scene, Dorothy had volunteered to look after her granddaughter while Claire worked. The arrangement had been beneficial for everyone, especially Claire.

Now, for the first time, Claire wondered if looking after a rather rambunctious child for the past seven years had taken its toll on her mother. Not that Claire hadn't taken responsibility for her Dani; she had, spending all her free time with the child and making sure Reginald and Dorothy had time to themselves.

From the moment she'd begun working for Reginald, she'd strived to be as independent as possible. Moving in with Dorothy and her stepfather had simply been a practical solution, but from the outset Claire had insisted on paying her own way, contributing to the running of the house, even paying her mother for looking after Dani.

At first Dorothy had been hurt that Claire wanted to pay her for looking after her beloved grandchild. But Claire had pointed out that if she and Dani had had to live elsewhere, she would have had to hire someone to look after Dani. This way, knowing Dani was being cared for under the watchful and loving eyes of her grandmother made Claire feel better about leaving Dani each day.

The emergency area was relatively quiet and a nurse smiled as she approached them.

'Could you tell me where I could find my wife, Dorothy Farmer?' Reginald asked, setting his luggage down next to a row of chairs. 'She was brought in earlier this evening,' he explained.

'Yes, Mr. Farmer,' the nurse replied.

'She's been moved to the third floor, room 320.'

'Is Dr. McGregor at the hospital?' Reginald asked.

'Yes, sir. I'll page him for you,' she said with a friendly smile.

Reginald turned to Claire. 'I can't stand here and wait. I'm going up to see Dorothy,' he said already moving toward the elevators.

'I'll wait for Bruce,' Claire said as the paging call for Dr. McGregor came over the public address system.

Behind her, Daniel crossed to the chairs and sat down. Claire glanced at him and she noted with surprise a look of tension flit across his handsome features. Dropping his suit jacket across his knees, he massaged his neck and combed his hands through his thick black hair in a gesture that spoke of tiredness.

Damn the man! Claire thought silently. She didn't want to feel sympathy for the man, she didn't want to feel anything for him, but somehow the lost and rather lonely look tugged at her heartstrings.

'Claire, you did manage to get a flight.'

Claire spun around to see Bruce McGregor emerge from an elevator nearby.

'You could say that,' Claire answered, and smiled in greeting.

'Where's Reginald?'

'He's gone up to see my mother,' Claire told him. 'How is she?'

'Resting,' Bruce said. 'And improving by the hour,' he added.

'And Dani? How is she? Where is she?' Claire wanted to know.

'Dani's just fine,' Bruce assured her. 'She's the one who called the ambulance, you know. You should be very proud of her. She did a great job. Come on, I'll take you to her. She's just down the hall in the first waiting room,' he added.

At his words Claire heard a sound behind her. She turned to find Daniel standing there watching her, his expression unreadable. Claire retraced her steps, closing the gap between them. 'Look . . . I think Dani's gone through enough for one night without adding to it by dropping another bombshell — ' She ground to a halt.

'Agreed,' Daniel cut in brusquely. 'I'm not totally insensitive,' he added, his voice controlled, the tension in him palpable.

Relief flowed through Claire at his response. 'Give me a few minutes alone with her, then I'll bring her out,' she suggested.

He held her gaze for a breathless second, those haunting gray eyes of his boring into hers, almost as if he were trying to see inside her soul. 'Okay,' he said.

She turned and followed Bruce down the corridor, aware all the while of Daniel's gaze on her at every step. The moment Bruce opened the waiting room door, however, Claire forgot Daniel, forgot everything but the child curled up on a couch, a pillow under her head and a blanket over her.

'I'll pop up to your mother's room and talk to Reginald,' Bruce said softly as she moved past him into the room.

'Thanks,' Claire murmured, and at the sound of both voices Dani sat up and pushed the blanket aside.

'Mommy! Mommy! You're back,' Dani cried as she hopped down from the couch and threw herself into her mother's arms.

Claire crouched and wrapped her arms around her daughter, hugging her tightly. Tears sprang to her eyes and she blinked them away, unwilling to let Dani see that she was upset. The traumatic events of the evening were over and Claire wanted to dwell on the positive rather than the negative aspects of what had happened.

'Hello, poppet!' Claire said into her daughter's shoulder-length brown curls, breathing in the sweet scent of her child. 'Dr. McGregor was just telling me that you did a wonderful job tonight. I'm very proud of you, darling,' Claire said as she held Dani at arm's length.

'I got to ride in the ambulance with Grandma,' Dani told her.

'Grandma was lucky you were there to look after her,' Claire said, her voice a little husky as she smiled at her daughter.

'Dr. Bruce told me that, too,' Dani said proudly. 'Grandma *is* going to be all right, just like Dr. Bruce said. She isn't going to die, is she?' she asked worriedly.

'No, my love. She isn't going to die,' Claire assured her daughter and was relieved to see the look of anxiety fade from her eyes.

'It was right after supper,' Dani said. 'I asked Grandma if she wanted me to help her with the dishes. But she didn't answer and she looked funny, like I do when I have a sore tummy.'

Claire nodded.

'I was scared, but then I remembered what the policeman said that time he came to our school. He said that in a 'mergency you dial the numbers 911 and tell the person on the other end your name and address. So that's what I did.'

'You did the right thing.' Claire smiled, her heart bursting with pride as she gently stroked Dani's cheek. Dani grinned, then suddenly her glance shifted to something over Claire's shoulder.

Claire knew instantly that it was Daniel. Taking a deep steadying breath she straightened and, grasping Dani's hand, turned to face him. Her heart jerked violently against her rib cage at the look of joy and wonder she could see in his eyes.

Daniel gazed at his daughter, drinking in the sight of her, noting every small detail from her head down to her toes. She looked like Claire, he decided as his eyes roamed over the child once more. Her hair was the same deep chestnut brown and she had the same heart-shaped face. But her eyes. Her eyes were gray like his.

'Hello. Who are you?' Dani asked.

'Hello.' Daniel pushed the word past lips that were dry. He could feel his heart pounding inside his chest, as if it were trying to escape, and he had to fight the overwhelming urge to run and gather this beautiful young creature that was his daughter into his arms.

'Dani, this is Daniel Hunter,' Claire said surprised at how calm she felt. 'He's a friend of mine, and the pilot who flew Grandpa Reg and I back from Vancouver,' she explained.

'You're a pilot — wow!' Dani said, her eyes wide, her gaze intent on Daniel.

'That's right,' her father replied.

'Can you take me for a ride in your plane?' Dani asked with a forthrightness that had Daniel smiling.

To the moon, he wanted to respond but curbed the impulse, glancing instead at Claire who was watching him closely, apprehension hovering in her cornflower-blue eyes.

'If it's all right with your mother,' Daniel said, shifting his attention back to his daughter, but not before he'd glimpsed the look of relief and gratitude that flashed in Claire's eyes at his answer.

Dani instantly turned to her mother. 'Can I, Mom? Please? Can I?' she pleaded, hopping up and down with excitement.

'May I,' Claire corrected automatically. 'I suppose ... ' she said reluctantly.

'Neato!' Dani said, bestowing a triumphant smile on Daniel, a smile that completely bowled him over, capturing his heart forever.

'Here you all are,' Reginald said as he appeared behind Daniel. 'Bruce told me I'd find you in here.'

'Grandpa.' Dani squealed in delight at the sight of her grandfather, and Daniel watched with envy as his daughter ran into Reginald's open arms. 'Did you see Grandma? She's going to be all right, isn't she?' Dani asked.

'She's going to be just fine,' Reginald

said. 'She's sleeping now,' he told her. 'That's why I left. She needs to rest.'

'Did you talk to her?' Claire asked.

'Only briefly,' came the reply. 'I told her we'd both managed to get a flight home and she seemed relieved. I think she was a bit worried about Dani,' he went on.

'I want to see her,' Claire said. 'But I don't want to wake her. Not if she's sleeping.'

'I told her we'd be back in the morning,' Reginald said.

'Can we go home now?' Dani asked.

'I think that's a good idea,' her grandfather responded. 'I asked the nurse at the desk to call a cab. It should be here by now. Let's go!'

Dani clutched Reginald's hand as they all made their way along the corridor. While the driver loaded their luggage into the trunk of the car, Claire and Daniel, with Dani between them, sat in the back seat while Reginald sat up front.

'Are you staying at our house, too?'

Dani asked her father as the taxi pulled out of the hospital driveway.

'Yes,' Daniel replied.

'Then can we go for a ride in your plane tomorrow?' Dani wanted to know.

Daniel threw Claire a quick glance. Now that he'd met his daughter he wasn't in any hurry to be separated from her. The need to get to know her, to spend time with her was like nothing he'd ever known before.

'Daniel, you're more than welcome to stay for a few days,' Reginald said from the front seat. 'In fact, there's an estate auction coming up next Saturday and there'll be a number of quality pieces up for auction. You're sure to find something of interest. Why don't you stick around and check it out? We'd be happy to have you,' Reginald assured him. 'Wouldn't we, Claire?'

5

Claire felt her body tense at her stepfather's question. The mere thought of having Daniel around for a week, living under the same roof, was already tying her stomach in knots.

'Mom, Grandpa asked you a question,' Dani said, gazing innocently up at her mother. 'Aren't you going to answer him?'

'Yes . . . sorry, Reg. I was daydreaming,' Claire replied. She turned to Daniel. 'By all means, stay,' she invited in a tone that barely disguised the sarcasm and anger she could feel simmering just beneath the surface.

But what could she say? She felt trapped just like a fox who'd been chased up a tree by hounds. There was no means of escape. Daniel's presence in Peachville posed a definite threat, not only to her peace of mind, but more importantly to the safe little world she'd built for herself and Dani.

She'd have liked nothing better than to accuse him of manipulating the circumstances to his advantage. But she'd stifled the impulse, knowing her stepfather would be shocked and hurt by her bad manners.

'I must say I'm tempted,' Daniel said, glancing again at Claire, noticing even in the dimly lit interior of the taxi, the look of annoyance as well as dismay that flickered across her features. 'But surely you have enough to contend with without adding a houseguest to the list,' he added, his conscience tugging at him a little.

'Not at all,' Reginald said magnanimously. 'Unless of course you have urgent business to attend to . . . '

'Nothing that can't wait,' Daniel replied, quickly making mental notes to reschedule the meetings his brother had set up for him in California for the following week. Paul would be annoyed, of course, but right now Daniel didn't care. All that mattered was that he'd be able to spend time with his daughter.

'Then, I repeat, we'd be happy to have you,' Reginald said easily.

'Thank you,' Daniel said graciously. He knew he was taking advantage of the situation, but he also knew that he'd be a fool to look a gift horse in the mouth.

'Can you take me flying tomorrow?' Dani's question cut through the tension hovering between the two adults in the back seat.

'Maybe we should wait a day or two,' Daniel suggested. During the landing earlier, one of the warning lights on the instrument panel had lit up. He'd noted it in the logbook and he'd meant to ask the mechanic to check it out, but they'd left the airfield in rather a hurry. Safety was the first priority and he had no intention flying anywhere until he'd had the problem looked at. 'You'll want to visit your grandmother tomorrow, won't you?' he said.

Dani nodded, trying with difficulty to

hide her disappointment. 'But you will take me flying one day, won't you?' she asked, gazing up at him once more.

Daniel felt his heart knock against his rib cage at the look of longing in his daughter's eyes. 'I promise,' he said solemnly, knowing that if she'd been asking him for the moon, somehow he'd have found a way to get it for her.

'Ah, here we are. Home at last,' Reginald said with a sigh as the taxi pulled into the driveway.

The large rambling old house at the top of the driveway was shrouded in darkness. The taxi came to a halt at the foot of the steps leading to the front door and Claire climbed out into the sultry night air.

'It looks awfully dark,' Dani said, inching closer to her mother.

'We'll soon have some lights on,' Claire responded as she took her daughter's hand and headed up the steps to the front door. Rummaging in her purse Claire located her key and in a matter of minutes she was inside, switching on the lights that lit up the front entrance and the driveway.

Dani moved past her and walked toward the kitchen. She stopped in the doorway and flicked on the light switch, revealing the supper dishes still on the table as well as a general disarray. Claire came up behind her.

'Grandma was right there in her chair,' Dani said, a faint quiver in her voice, the memory of those traumatic moments earlier in the evening returning and obviously having an effect on her.

Claire put her hands on Dani's shoulders and gave her a gentle squeeze. 'It's all over now, darling. You did exactly the right thing and Grandma is going to be fine,' she said. 'Come on, let's go upstairs and get you into your nightie. It's way past your bedtime,' she added, silently wishing she could somehow wipe those frightening moments from Dani's mind.

She knew they would fade in time, but she knew, too, that it was important for Dani to talk about what happened in order to deal with the trauma she'd experienced.

'Will you read me a story?' Dani asked, switching topics.

'It's very late. Nearly eleven-thirty . . .' Claire pointed out, suddenly feeling tired herself.

'A little one? Please . . . ' Dani pleaded in a voice that could have belonged to a three-year-old and Claire realized Dani simply wanted her mother to stay with her for a while.

Claire bent to kiss the top of her daughter's head. 'All right,' she said. 'But just a short one,' she added, knowing that once Dani was in bed she'd undoubtedly be asleep in a matter of minutes.

As mother and daughter headed toward the stairs, Reginald and Daniel, each carrying some luggage, came through the front door. 'Off to bed are you, poppet?' Reginald said as he set the bags down.

Dani nodded then tried to stifle a

yawn. 'Night,' she mumbled, managing a weak smile.

'Good night, Dani,' Reginald and Daniel replied in unison.

'I'll be down in a few minutes,' Claire said.

'No problem,' Reginald said. 'In view of all that's happened tonight, I could use a nightcap,' he went on. 'Will you join me, Daniel?'

'Don't mind if I do,' he replied, lingering for a moment longer until his daughter disappeared from sight, before turning and following Reginald into the living room.

Ten minutes later Claire rejoined the men as they sat sipping brandy.

'That didn't take long,' Reginald commented. 'Would you like something to drink?'

'Dani fell asleep almost before her head hit the pillow,' Claire told him. 'And . . . no thank you, Reg, I don't want anything. I'm too tired,' she replied before turning to Daniel. 'I'll show you the guest room now, if you're ready.'

Daniel quickly drained the brandy from his glass and set it on the coffee table in front of him. 'Excellent brandy, Reg. Thank you,' he said, getting to his feet. 'And thanks again for your hospitality.'

Reginald smiled and nodded, lifting his own glass in acknowledgment of Daniel's words.

Claire led the way from the living room and crossed to the stairs. She climbed the first two steps but stopped when she realized Daniel had made a short detour to the front door to retrieve a small black bag sitting amid the luggage.

'I always carry an overnight bag in the jet in case of emergencies,' Daniel told her. In three strides he had caught up to her and Claire felt her pulse skip crazily for a moment in reaction to his nearness.

She turned abruptly and started up the stairs, her aim simply to put some distance between them, but in her haste her toe caught on the carpeted stairway.

She would have fallen, but Daniel, with lightning reflexes, grabbed her arm and held her steady.

'Careful,' he said, before releasing her.

'Thanks,' Claire mumbled. Where his fingers had gripped her arm there lingered a tingling heat she wished she could ignore, and she could also feel her face grow warm with embarrassment.

At the top of the stairs she turned right, coming to a halt at the first door. 'The bedroom is quite small,' she told him as she entered the room. 'But like most of them in the house, it has its own bathroom,' she added as she pointed to the door on the other side of the room.

'It's great — thank you,' Daniel said, tossing his bag onto the bed.

Claire had described the room as small but with Daniel's tall imposing figure taking up much of the space, it seemed to have shrunk in size, and it was all she could do to squeeze past him and retreat out of harm's way.

'I'll say good-night,' Claire said, her hand on the door-knob.

'Claire, wait! Before you go, there's something I want to say . . . ' Daniel began, and hearing the hesitancy and anxiety lacing his tone, Claire lifted her gaze to meet his. 'Dani . . . my daughter . . . our daughter . . . she's absolutely beautiful,' he said with sincerity, his gray eyes sparkling with both pride and love. 'She's a warm, caring, loving child,' he continued. 'You've done a terrific job. You must be very proud of her.'

'Thank you,' she murmured huskily, immeasurably moved by his words. Whatever she'd expected, it certainly hadn't been words of praise. She could still recall his anger when she'd accused him of not caring about his daughter, but he'd obviously put that aside; she couldn't help but admire the way he'd handled his first meeting with Dani.

As she closed the door behind her she was suddenly bombarded with feelings of guilt. Slowly she made her way down the hall, stopping in front of Dani's bedroom, its door directly opposite her own.

Claire tiptoed across the carpeted floor to the bed and gazed down at the sleeping child. For the most part, Dani had been a happy, contented baby, but there had been times during Dani's preschool years that Claire had despaired at the job of raising a daughter on her own.

Not that she'd been entirely on her own. Without the love and support she'd received from her mother and Reginald, Claire doubted she'd have survived Dani's terrible twos.

Stroking a lock of hair off Dani's face, Claire bent to kiss the pink cheek, and with a sigh silently withdrew. Crossing the hall into her own room she left her bedroom door ajar as she always did, in case Dani should need her.

Taking a cotton nightdress from the dresser drawer, Claire entered her own bathroom. After completing her bedtime ritual, she switched off the light and climbed into bed.

When she'd come upstairs with Dani, she'd opened their bedroom windows wide in the hope of creating a cooling breeze. But tonight the breeze was nonexistent and the air felt hot and oppressive.

Her skin felt damp and sticky as she lay staring at the ceiling, and those feelings of guilt she'd been trying hard to suppress bubbled to the surface once more, bringing with them the questions that had plagued her since her return from her disastrous trip to Boston when Dani was only six weeks old.

Should she have been more assertive that day and insisted on seeing Daniel, wedding day or not? What would his reaction have been? Would he have welcomed her and Dani with open arms? Would he have called off his wedding? Had she been wrong to keep Dani's existence a secret from her father?

She'd asked herself these questions countless times, but the answers always varied. Over the years her guilt had diminished, and she'd simply gone on with the business of making a life for herself and Dani. Whenever the doubts started rolling in she'd reminded herself that Daniel had been the one who'd broken his promise to meet her in Paris, walking out of her life without even saying goodbye.

Fool! Pathetic, romantic fool! But she only had herself to blame, falling head over heels in love with a handsome stranger. She'd been stupidly naive to think her feelings had been returned. She'd believed Daniel had been as deeply in love with her as she'd been with him, convinced that fate had brought them together on that early August night on a moonlit beach on the shores of the Mediterranean.

Claire felt the hot, wet tears slide into her hair as a pain clutched at her insides. The memories she'd thought were safely locked away, the memories of those unforgettable days they'd spent together, began to replay inside her head.

* * *

The fact that the tour bus carrying twenty-five students from several Canadian universities had made it as far as the village of Camiore, had been due solely to the driver. Though the village sported two small hotels, there was no garage and no mechanic. After a quick evaluation, the driver declared that the problem was in the transmission and it would take several days to fix.

After changing into shorts and a bikini top in the hotel room she was to share with two other students, Claire, tired of the lack of privacy, had wandered off alone to explore the sandy beach that seemed to stretch forever.

She walked a good distance from the village, stopping once to watch the huge red ball that was the sun, slide below the horizon to the west to be replaced in the sky by an enormous silver moon almost equally as bright.

She wasn't sure how long she'd been staring out across the water that shimmered like a bed of diamonds in the moonlight, when all at once she saw a man walk out of the waves. Startled, she'd stood rooted to the spot as the figure, water streaming from his bronzed naked body, walked up the beach toward her.

For a heart-stopping minute she'd thought she was seeing things, but as the man drew closer, his muscular body glistening in the silvery light, she'd felt her heart shudder in her breast and an unfamiliar heat slowly unfurl somewhere in the center of her being, to spread with tingling awareness to every cell.

'You're trespassing,' the apparition said, the sound of his deep rich voice sending her blood sizzling through her veins.

'You're naked,' she replied throatily, too mesmerized by his appearance to comment on the fact that he was undoubtedly American.

Laughter rumbled from his lips, intensifying the sensations skimming along her nerve endings. 'I know. But this is a private beach,' he said as he bent to pick up a towel he'd undoubtedly left on the sand prior to his swim. He proceeded to dry himself, unaware of the havoc he was causing to her senses.

'I didn't see any signs,' Claire responded, totally mesmerized by his actions, her fingers suddenly itching to touch him, to trace the outline of his broad shoulders, to explore the flat plane that was his stomach and to feel the texture of his skin.

'Can you read Italian?' he asked as he tossed the towel across his shoulder and casually retrieved a pair of cutoffs from the sand.

'No,' she answered, unable to tear her eyes away as he stepped into the shorts and pulled them on.

'That would explain it,' he said, a

hint of humor in his voice now.

Claire lifted her gaze to meet his. Gray eyes, the color of a stormy sea, held hers captive for several long moments. Her heart jolted against her rib cage and her lungs forgot how to function as he calmly and coolly let his eyes roam over her from head to toe.

'So, tell me . . . who are you? And what are you doing in Camiore?' he asked as he began to dry his hair with the towel.

'My name is Claire MacInnes and I'm traveling through Europe with a group of students. Only, our tour bus broke down,' she told him. 'Who are you and what are you doing here?' she asked a trifle breathlessly, surprised by her own boldness, wanting only to prolong the meeting, and at the very least learn the name of this devastatingly handsome stranger.

His smile sent her heart into a fresh tailspin and she knew in that moment she was lost.

'I'm Daniel Hunter,' he said. 'I'm

staying at the villa on the hillside, behind you,' he told her, nodding in its direction. 'It belongs to a friend of mine.'

'Wow!' Claire turned, instantly noticing the outline of an enormous house, its lights twinkling in the moonlight. 'Must be nice to have friends who own a villa,' she commented as she turned to face him once more.

'Yes, it is,' he replied, easily. 'Actually, they've gone to Rome for a few days. If you'd like a look around the place, why don't you drop by tomorrow, sometime. I doubt your bus will have been fixed by then. Bring a few of your student friends with you, if you like,' he added before slowly moving toward the path leading over the sand dune.

'Thanks. I might just do that,' she said, and stood watching until he was out of sight.

The following morning, Claire waited until her roommates had gone down to breakfast before she slipped from the hotel and headed for the villa. She'd spent the night tossing and turning, her dreams filled with erotic images of Daniel Hunter. When she'd returned to the hotel the night before, her companions hadn't bothered to ask where she'd been, they'd simply passed on the news the tour leader had told them to enjoy the unscheduled break, which might last three or four days.

Claire had decided that if three days was all she had, she wanted to spend them with Daniel Hunter. When she knocked on the door of the villa half an hour later, she'd expected a servant to answer, but to her surprise and pleasure, Daniel appeared.

His smile of welcome sent her pulse racing madly. After showing her through the beautiful house, he invited her to join him for a swim. This time he wore a bathing suit, but seeing him in the scant cloth, Claire couldn't help thinking he looked even sexier than he had the night before.

The morning went by in a kind of daze. They swam together, then lay under the shade of the trees while she told him of all the towns the tour had visited. They walked back to the villa where Daniel prepared a lunch of a green salad, a variety of cheeses and some freshly baked buns from the bakery in the village.

After lunch they'd dozed off in the lounge chairs on the shaded patio and by late afternoon Claire felt as if she'd known him forever and she never wanted to leave. When Daniel suggested they walk into Camiore and eat at the small restaurant there, she'd readily agreed. They were shown to a secluded table that afforded a spectacular view of the water.

Claire couldn't remember a single thing she ate; all she remembered was the way Daniel's eyes crinkled when he smiled at her, the sensuous curve of his mouth and the way his eyes sparkled with humor and something more, something she couldn't quite decipher.

As they walked back along the beach to the villa, Daniel took her hand in his and Claire felt as if she were walking on air. She'd never experienced such overpowering emotions, such a depth of longing, never truly understood the meaning of sexual awareness until now. Being with Daniel awakened emotions that were both frightening and incredibly exciting.

They hadn't gone very far when Daniel came to a halt. When he turned her to face him she felt sure he was going to kiss her, and her heart took a giant leap as she waited with heady anticipation for his lips to touch hers.

'I think we'd better call it a night,' he said softly.

'But I'm not tired,' she replied, knowing she sounded childish but unable to stop herself. She didn't want to leave him, never wanted to leave him.

'Claire . . . ' Her name was a sigh on his lips. 'This is moving too fast, even for me,' he said, a hint of regret in his voice.

'But — ' She began, before he silenced her with a kiss that, even though it lasted a little more than a second, succeeded in capturing her heart.

He took several steps back. 'Go! Now!' he ordered in a voice that allowed no room for argument.

Claire felt tears prick her eyes and her vision clouded as she began to turn and walk away. Her body ached with disappointment and frustration and she'd only taken a half-dozen steps when she stopped and sank to the sand hugging her knees, trying to soothe her bruised heart.

She wasn't sure how long she sat there feeling sorry for herself. She thought a swim might help to alleviate the tension still singing through her, and so she slithered out of the sundress she'd worn that morning and ran naked into the surf. The cool water on her skin was like a sweet caress and she began to stroke through the breaking waves to where she and Daniel had been swimming earlier in the day.

Moonlight danced on the water and

she flipped onto her back staring up at the night sky, lazily counting the stars as they appeared. Without warning, a stronger wave washed over her, pushing her under and dragging her down.

Struggling to hold her breath, she frantically tried to fight the current that kept pulling her beneath the surface. It had happened so quickly that in a matter of seconds her lungs felt as if they were about to burst.

All at once a strong arm encircled her, to hold on tightly, before hauling her to the surface, where she was at last able to inhale several mouthfuls of life-sustaining air. Claire knew instantly her rescuer was Daniel, and as a result her feelings of panic subsided. She relaxed against him, saying a silent prayer of thanks.

When she felt her heels touch the sand, she tried to stand up. But before she could right herself, Daniel swung her effortlessly into his arms and began walking out of the water and across the warm sand. He carried her up the beach to the shelter of the dunes before gently lowering her legs onto the sand.

Her breath caught in her throat as her body brushed against his and she realized he, too, was naked. Already weak from her frightening encounter in the water, she stumbled against him. As his arms tightened around her, she felt as if she were being dragged under by a new and more powerful undertow as she experienced for the first time in her life, the quick sharp edge of desire as it vibrated through her with a staggering force.

Daniel's jaw gently grazed her cheek and she closed her eyes, giving herself up to the wonder of being held in his arms. She took a shaky breath and succeeded in bombarding her already overstimulated senses with the erotic male scent of him.

Slowly, agonizingly, she pulled away. As she did, her mouth feathered a caress against his cheek. She heard his sharp intake of breath and felt his whole body grow taut with tension.

Suddenly his hands grabbed her upper arms as if he intended to thrust her away from him.

For a heart-stopping moment their gazes met and held, and Claire saw the look of raw desire that flashed in his gray eyes a split second before his mouth swooped down to claim hers in a kiss that rocked her very soul.

★ ★ ★

Claire woke with a start, her legs entangled in the bed sheets. Her heart was hammering against her breastbone in frenzied reaction to the memories washing over her.

She swore under her breath and, kicking the sheets aside, she sat on the edge of the bed and waited for her heartbeat to return to normal. It had been a long time since she'd indulged in a trip down memory lane, and she knew without a doubt that Daniel's reappearance in her life had everything to do with her agitated state of mind.

Eight years ago she'd thought she'd found the man of her dreams, the man with whom she could share her life. But the dream had died, leaving only the bitter taste of ashes.

Rising from the bed, Claire made her way to her daughter's room. Somehow she always felt reassured and comforted staring down at Dani's cherublike features. While the emotional cost of raising a child without a father had been high, she knew if she had to do it all over again she wouldn't hesitate, not for a second.

A sound captured her attention and she glanced around. Her pulse kicked into high gear when she recognized Daniel's tall muscular frame silhouetted in the doorway. Claire ran a nervous hand through her disheveled hair and she licked her dry lips.

That he was naked from the waist up was obvious and Claire felt her pulse pick up speed in reaction. Go away! she wanted to shout at him. She had enough to deal with. The dream that

144

had awakened her a short time ago was still too fresh in her mind.

'Is Dani all right?' he asked in a whisper.

'She's fine,' Claire said softly as she closed the gap between them, worried that their voices would waken Dani.

'I thought I heard someone cry out,' he said, turning his body at an angle to let her through, but making no attempt to return to the guest room.

Claire came to a halt in the doorway, nerves jittering, all too aware of the man standing a scant few inches away.

'I used to have nightmares sometimes, when I was a child,' Daniel said softly, 'usually if I'd been watching a scary movie,' he added.

His breath fanned Claire's face, causing her stomach muscles to tighten and her heart to trip over itself in startled response. She watched in fascination as he glanced at the sleeping figure of his daughter, his sensuous mouth curving into a smile.

He turned to face Claire once more.

'You know, I still can't believe she's my daughter.' His words were little more than a throaty whisper, yet there was no mistaking the wonder and pride in his voice.

A warmth stole over her at the sheer honesty of his remark and she wondered, not for the first time, if she'd made the wrong decision when she'd decided not to tell him about Dani.

She met his gaze and saw in the depths of his gray eyes a hope and a longing that tugged strangely at her heart. She swayed toward him, pulled by an invisible force older than time itself.

But suddenly sanity prevailed. 'No!' The word burst forth from somewhere deep inside, and with a muffled cry she tore herself away, scurrying like a frightened mouse for the sanctuary of her room.

She closed the door behind her and leaned heavily against it, waiting for her heartbeat to slow and her body to stop shaking. Damn the man! She hugged herself tightly, trying with difficulty to erase the memory of those moments when she'd almost given in to what was simply her baser instincts.

Why did he have to be so damned attractive? It wasn't fair that his nearness affected her so profoundly, but that's how it had been from the first moment she'd met him. She'd been eighteen then, a teenager with raging hormones. She could blame her youth and inexperience with the opposite sex for the predicament she'd landed in.

But now that same excuse didn't apply. She was a mature woman, a single parent with a career she loved and a child she adored, and she neither needed nor wanted a man to make her feel complete.

Daniel's reappearance in her life was something she'd have to deal with. She'd just have to keep him at a distance, that was all. And maybe the novelty of being a father would wear off. And maybe Daniel would return to Boston and let them get on with their lives. And maybe pigs would fly!

6

Claire dozed fitfully for the remainder of the night but at six-thirty, as the morning sunlight peeked through her bedroom curtains, she rose and headed for the shower. As the water cascaded over her, the memory of the previous night — her dream and her encounter with Daniel in the hallway — returned.

Her heart skipped several beats and reluctantly she acknowledged that he was still the most devastatingly attractive man she'd ever known.

Eight years ago when he'd charmed and seduced her into a brief but unforgettable liaison, she'd believed he'd shared her feelings. But not once during those incredible days had he ever spoken the three words that every woman in love longs to hear. And no wonder, the plain truth was that socialite Kelly Albright had been waiting for him back in Boston, a fact Claire had had confirmed when she'd read the details of his wedding in the society pages of the Boston newspaper on her flight back to Vancouver. A wedding of such magnitude, she hastened to remind herself, had to have been planned for some considerable time — at the very least, a year.

It had been during her brief but highly emotional stay at the hospital after Dani's birth that she'd made the decision to at least try to track Daniel down. Each day outside the hospital nursery she'd watch the group of new fathers come to the window to gaze with pride and wonder at their newborn infants, and each day her feelings of guilt intensified.

Finding Daniel had proved far easier than she'd anticipated. A month after she'd brought Dani home from the hospital, Claire had been browsing through a pile of Reginald's trade magazines and catalogs on various antique auctions and sales held throughout the country, when she'd suddenly found herself staring at a photograph of Daniel amid a group of dealers attending a charity auction in New York.

As a result she'd made a number of discreet inquiries, finally locating his home address in Boston, and before her courage had failed her she'd called a travel agent and booked a flight.

The trip had been an unmitigated disaster, and on her return she'd firmly and resolutely closed the door on the past. But now a twist of fate had brought Daniel back into her life. And while Claire accepted the fact that he had a right to get to know his own daughter, she was unwilling to tell her daughter the truth, refusing to place Dani in a situation where she could be hurt.

Besides, she had little reason to trust Daniel. He'd walked out of her life once before, and he could just as easily do it again.

With a sigh Claire rinsed the last of the shampoo from her hair and turned off the water. She stepped from the shower and after wrapping her wet hair in a towel, she used another to dry off.

Reentering her bedroom, Claire crossed to the dresser and pulled out a pair of blue cotton shorts and a blue-and-white short-sleeved shirt. She dressed quickly, and after towel drying her hair, finished the process with her hair dryer. Her hair had a natural curl, making it relatively easy to style, and Claire much preferred the shorter, more manageable length.

Checking that Dani was still asleep, Claire quietly made her way downstairs. She'd been too tired last night to clean up the kitchen, but she didn't want Dani to come down and find things in the same state of disorder.

It didn't take her long to rinse the dishes and put them in the dishwasher. As she finished scooping coffee into the automatic coffeemaker, she was joined by her stepfather, wearing the dressing gown her mother had given him for his birthday less than a month ago.

'Morning, Claire,' Reginald greeted

her. 'Coffee on?'

'Yes. It'll be ready in a few minutes,' Claire replied, noticing the lines of worry and weariness on his features. 'How are you feeling this morning?' she asked.

'Tired. I didn't sleep very well,' he said, pulling out a chair from the table and sitting down.

'Me, either,' she said, moving to stand behind him. She put her hands on his shoulders and dropped a kiss on the bald spot on the top of his head. 'Mom's going to be fine. Try not to worry,' she urged gently.

Reginald reached up to pat her hand. 'I just wish I'd been here for her.' He sighed. 'Your mother needed me, Claire, and I let her down,' he said.

'Don't be silly,' Claire scolded, her heart aching for him. 'You mustn't blame yourself. We've all been taking her for granted, assuming she's invincible,' she said. 'We just have to be thankful she'll be all right, and make sure we all heed the warning.'

'You're right,' he said, managing to give her a wan smile. 'And I intend to ensure that I never let her down again. She means the world to me — ' he broke off, emotion clouding his voice.

'I know, Reg,' Claire said, touched by his confession. 'And believe me, since the two of you have been together, I've never seen her happier.' She blinked back the tears suddenly stinging her eyes, realizing that the night could have had an entirely different outcome. 'Would you like breakfast?' she asked, wanting to divert their thoughts from what might have happened.

'Thanks, but I'm not hungry. Coffee will be fine,' he replied. 'Do you think it's too early to call the hospital?' he asked, rising from the table.

'Of course not,' Claire assured him. She turned and extracted a coffee mug from one of the kitchen cupboards. 'Take this with you,' she said as she filled the mug and handed it to him.

'Thanks,' he said. 'After I make the

call, I'll get dressed and head over to the hospital.'

'Dani should be awake soon,' Claire said. 'We can all go.'

Reginald nodded and headed to his office. Claire poured herself a cup of coffee. She couldn't remember ever seeing her stepfather this upset before. Last night he'd seemed calm and in control, but he'd obviously been putting up a brave front.

The sound of someone running down the stairs brought Claire instantly alert, and she glanced up to see Dani, still wearing her nightie, come racing into the kitchen.

'Good morning!' Claire smiled at her daughter.

'Hi, Mom,' Dani replied. 'I'm hungry,' she announced as she pulled her chair away from the table and climbed onto it. 'Can I have a banana cut up in my cereal?' she asked.

'Sure,' Claire said, already pulling a cereal bowl from the shelf nearby. 'You get the cereal and I'll get the milk,' she suggested, turning around to open the fridge door.

'Okay,' Dani responded as she hopped down from her chair. 'May I have a glass of orange juice, too?'

'Yes,' Claire replied, reaching for the carton of juice.

'Oh, hello.' Dani's greeting alerted Claire to Daniel's arrival, and she felt her body grow tense. 'I'm having cereal. Want some?' Dani asked.

'Hello, yourself,' Daniel responded. 'Cereal would be nice. Thanks,' he added, a warmth stealing over him at the friendly smile his daughter had bestowed on him. He wondered for a moment if there was some way to patent her smile. There was certainly something magical about it, he thought as he sat down beside her at the table.

'Good morning,' Claire greeted him calmly, glad to have had Dani's warning, which had given her a few extra seconds to school her features into a polite smile. She deliberately ignored the way her heart began to trip a little faster at the sight of him, looking cool and relaxed in a pair of baggy cotton slacks and shirt, his black hair still wet from the shower.

'And a beautiful morning it is,' Daniel replied, noting Claire's rather forced smile. She seemed tense and a little nervous, and he supposed, under the circumstances, that was to be expected.

Since the trauma of the night before, he'd pushed everything else aside, but he was determined to confront Claire about a number of things. And the sooner the better.

When she'd accused him in the restaurant of not caring about his daughter, he'd snapped. He'd thought he'd finally come to grips with the guilt he'd been living with since the death of his son, but somehow her comment had reopened the wounds inflicted by the loss of his child, and like a bear with a sore paw, he'd lashed out.

He'd cared deeply about Kevin, more deeply than he'd thought possible. But caring hadn't been enough to keep his son alive, or for that matter save a marriage doomed from the outset.

And the reason he hadn't asked about his daughter was because he'd scarcely had time to grasp the true significance of the momentous news. To learn he was a father, to be told that he had a seven-year-old, healthy child, had overwhelmed him.

But while he understood Claire's caution, he wanted to reassure her that he didn't plan to take any drastic action, that she had nothing to fear in that direction. All he wanted was a chance to get to know his daughter, to become a part of her life, to make up for the years he'd already missed.

At the moment the situation was a rather delicate one, but one thing he intended to be firm about was that Dani be told the truth. He didn't know what explanation or information Claire had given Dani regarding her father, but he planned to find out.

'Would you like a banana in your

cereal, too?' Dani's question cut through Daniel's musings.

'Mmm . . . that's a good idea,' Daniel replied, accepting the fruit Dani handed him.

As he peeled the banana and sliced it onto his cereal, Daniel was suddenly reminded of the summer days of his own childhood spent with his grandparents at their cottage on the shores of Lake Ontario. Every July, he and his brother, Paul, would travel to the cottage and stay until late August.

Daniel's grandmother's kitchen, similar in many ways to this one, had also been bright and cozy. And one of his strongest memories was of the atmosphere of warmth, love and security that had surrounded them there. He could feel it here in this room and found himself admiring Claire for having created such a positive and loving environment for their child to grow up in.

How he envied Claire those years with Dani, watching each stage of her growth from infant to toddler to child, and not for the first time he wondered why she hadn't contacted him when she'd learned of her pregnancy. That question and a hundred others were simmering in his head and he vowed he'd have the answers soon.

'Where do you live?' Dani asked him through a mouthful of flakes.

'Boston,' Daniel replied.

'Where's that?'

'Way on the other side of the country,' Daniel told her.

'Are you married?' Dani continued as she munched down on a piece of banana.

Daniel tried hard not to chuckle. 'Not anymore. I'm divorced,' he said.

'My friend Caroline's parents are 'vorced,' Dani said, stumbling over the word. 'Her dad lives in Vancouver now and Caroline visits him every month. She's lucky 'cause she gets to do lots of neat things when she's with her dad. I wish I had a dad to do stuff with,' Dani declared with a sigh.

Claire almost choked on her coffee at her daughter's words. Caroline had made several trips to Vancouver and ever since, she'd been bragging to Dani about the fun she had with her father. Dani, no doubt a little jealous of her friend, had decided she needed to find herself a father, one with whom she could do special things, just like Caroline.

As a result, for the past few months, any male acquaintance of Claire's who wasn't already married, had come under scrutiny as a possible candidate for the job. Claire, had chosen to ignore her daughter's somewhat harmless attempts to find a father. Until now, that is.

But before she could make a comment, Reginald, dressed in casual slacks and a short-sleeved shirt, and looking a little brighter, joined them in the kitchen.

'Did you call the hospital? How's Mom this morning?' Claire asked, glad to be able to divert the conversation away from the current topic.

'Morning,' Reginald said. Nodding to Daniel, he patted Dani's head as he came around the table. 'I called the hospital and talked to one of the night nurses who was just going off duty. She assured me Dorothy spent a restful night.'

'That's wonderful,' Claire said brightly, relieved by the news.

'Grandma's feeling better?' Dani said, her gray eyes intent on her grandfather.

'Much better,' Reginald said, flashing his granddaughter a reassuring smile. 'The nurse mentioned that there's no restrictions as far as visiting hours are concerned. We can go anytime.'

'Can I come, too?' Dani wanted to know, glancing anxiously at her mother.

'Of course. We can go right after you've finished breakfast,' Reginald replied. 'You're welcome to come along, too, Daniel,' he added.

'Thanks, Reg,' Daniel acknowledged. 'I'll accept a ride into town, but I won't intrude on your family visit,' he went on. 'If I'm going to stay for that estate sale you mentioned, there are a few items I need to pick up. Perhaps I can do that while you visit your wife. Then I can meet you back at the hospital when I'm finished.'

'By all means,' Reginald said, refilling his coffee mug from the carafe.

'Oh, would you mind if I used my calling card and made a few telephone calls?' Daniel asked as he rose from the table and crossed to the sink to deposit his empty cereal bowl.

'Not at all,' Reginald said. 'If you want a little privacy, you can use the phone in my office,' he added. 'Come, I'll show you where it is.'

'I'll just help myself to a mug of coffee first. If I may?' Daniel replied, turning to Claire who stood rigidly beside him.

Claire quickly extracted a mug from the cupboard and held it out to him. The fact that Daniel was standing only a few inches away was having an adverse affect on her pulse. As he took the mug from her, their fingers made fleeting contact, and it was all she could do not to jerk her hand away.

Her eyes flew to meet his and for a heart-stopping moment the air between them was charged with electricity. She saw a flash of surprise and something more, something she couldn't easily define flicker briefly in his eyes before he dropped his gaze and proceeded nonchalantly to fill the mug with coffee.

'Mommy, can I have more juice, please?' Dani asked, effectively defusing the tension vibrating through Claire, tension due solely to Daniel's proximity.

'Of course,' Claire said, moving to open the fridge. Picking up the juice container, she crossed to the table, noticing with some relief that Daniel was already making his way from the kitchen.

Several minutes later Claire shooed Dani upstairs to dress, but as she cleared away the breakfast dishes she kept glancing over her shoulder expecting Daniel to reappear.

That he still had the power to stir her senses and create havoc within her was evident by her body's involuntary reaction each time he touched her, or for that matter, each time he came anywhere near her. He'd broken her heart once, and she was determined that she wasn't going to fall victim to his charm a second time.

'Will Grandma be coming home with us?' Dani asked as Claire drove the car away from the house half an hour later.

'I don't know,' Claire replied. 'That's a question we can ask Dr. McGregor when we see him,' she said. 'Why?'

''Cause Grandma promised to take me swimming at Rainbow Lake,' Dani explained. 'We were going to have a picnic lunch, then pick you and Grandpa up at the airport.'

'Well, we'll just have to see,' Claire said. 'But even if Grandma does get home with us today, I doubt she'll feel like taking a trip to Rainbow Lake.'

'Couldn't you take me?' Dani persisted.

'We'll decide later. Besides, summer isn't over yet. There'll be lots of other days for a picnic,' Claire said, not wanting to make a promise she couldn't keep.

Dani slouched down in her seat and said nothing. It wasn't difficult to read frustration and disappointment in her daughter's demeanor. Claire understood that Dani didn't fully understand the severity of what had happened to her grandmother, but she knew, too, that Dani would soon get tired of sulking.

Twenty minutes later, Claire pulled the car into the hospital parking lot.

'If you'll point me in the direction of the main street, I'll be on my way,' Daniel said once they'd crossed to the hospital's front entrance.

'When you get to the end of this block, make a right turn. Main Street is two blocks straight ahead,' Claire told him.

'That sounds easy enough,' Daniel said. 'I'll meet you back here in . . . say an hour. And, Reg, please give your wife my best wishes for a speedy recovery.'

'Thank you, Daniel. I will,' Reginald said and, taking Dani's hand in his, he turned and walked into the building.

Claire made to follow but Daniel put his hand on her arm to detain her. Her skin tingled at the touch and she felt her pulse begin to accelerate a split second before she broke contact.

'I know this isn't the time or the place, but we need to talk,' Daniel said.

'You're right, this isn't the time,' she told him coolly, annoyance rippling through her. Right now her main concern was her mother, and Claire was eager to see for herself that Dorothy was indeed all right.

'Believe me, Claire, I'm not going anywhere. I'm staying right here in Peachville, at least until we reach some kind of compromise regarding my daughter,' he told her. 'You'd be wise to accept that,' he added, an edge to his voice now.

He held her gaze for what seemed an eternity, as if he were trying to imprint his words on her brain. 'Ignoring me won't work. We'll talk sooner or later. You can count on it,' he said before striding away.

Claire drew a shaky breath as she watched him leave. He was right about one thing, she acknowledged as she turned to follow Reginald and Dani. She couldn't ignore him, had never been able to ignore him, or fully understand her reaction to him.

And even after eight long years the yearning to feel the tantalizing caress of his hand, to know again the quick sharp stab of desire as his mouth devoured hers, to experience the wild and wonderful sensations only he could arouse, was almost more than she could bear.

Claire slowed to a halt, suddenly fighting back the moan of anguish threatening to break free. She bit down on the inner softness of her mouth, glad of the pain that helped to distract her thoughts from the dangerous road they'd taken.

'Mom . . . quick!' Dani's voice startled her and she glanced up to see her daughter waving to her from the elevators.

Claire picked up her pace, slipping into the elevator a few seconds before the doors closed, but as the car made its slow ascent she found herself wondering if life would ever be the same.

A few minutes later when Claire entered her mother's hospital room, she was shocked to see how pale and tired her mother looked. Though Dorothy Farmer's eyes lit up at the sight of them trooping into her room, Claire could see the fear and the strain behind her mother's smile.

'It's so good to see you,' her mother said as she smiled lovingly at Reginald who'd approached the bed to kiss his wife.

'Are you really better now, Grandma?' Dani asked, releasing her grip on Claire's fingers and crossing to her grandmother's bedside.

'Yes, darling, I'm much better' came the reply as she held out her hand to the child. 'Thanks to you,' she added, squeezing Dani's hand.

'I wanted to come up and see you last night, Mom, but Reg said you were sleeping,' Claire told her as she joined Dani and bent to kiss her mother's cheek. 'You gave us all a fright,' she added as she blinked back the tears pricking her eyes.

'I know,' Dorothy responded, managing a weak smile. 'And I can't tell you what a comfort it was to see Reg walk in here last night. I wasn't sure I'd ever — ' she broke off, and shook her head, trying with obvious difficulty not to cry.

'You're not going to cry are you, Grandma?' Dani asked, looking anxiously at her grandmother.

'Of course she's not going to cry,'

Reginald said, smiling at his wife as he gently squeezed her hand.

'There's a man staying at our house,' Dani said. 'He's the man who flied the plane that brought Grandpa and Mommy home,' she explained. 'And he's promised to take me for a ride one day while he's here,' she proudly told her grandmother.

'That sounds rather exciting,' Dorothy said. 'Tell me who is this Good Samaritan. Does he have a name? Do I know him?' she asked her husband.

'You may have heard me mention Daniel's name before,' Reginald said.

'Daniel?' his wife said, flashing Claire a frowning glance.

'Yes. Daniel Hunter,' her husband explained. 'His family owns Hunter Antiques in Boston. I haven't seen Daniel for a number of years. But we ran into him at the auction in Vancouver and he was kind enough to offer the use of his jet when he learned what had happened.'

'Did you say Daniel Hunter?' Dorothy asked, her eyes were riveted on Claire, who could see the confusion and concern clouding her mother's expression.

But before Reginald could answer, there was a knock at the door and Dr. McGregor poked his head in.

'Good morning.' He greeted everyone as he came into the room and crossed immediately to his patient. 'I see your entire family is here, Mrs. Farmer,' he said.

'I hope that's all right,' Dorothy said, somewhat anxiously.

'It's fine,' Bruce quickly assured her. 'But we don't want to overdo things. You need to rest and keep excitement at a minimum,' he cautioned. 'You have to look on this episode as a warning and heed it,' he went on.

'How long will she have to stay in hospital?' Reginald asked.

'Until the end of the week,' the doctor replied. 'That way I can run a few tests and keep an eye on her, just to make sure she doesn't do too much. Some patients feel better once they get home then quickly fall back into old habits and routines,' he explained. 'Right now my prescription for you, dear lady, is rest, rest, rest and no undue stress whatsoever. And I think that can be better accomplished if you stay here.'

'Then that's settled,' Claire quickly said. 'Because we only want what's best for you,' she added, smiling at her mother.

'But will you manage? I mean . . . ' her mother began, flashing Claire a worried glance.

'Dorothy, my love, didn't you hear what Dr. McGregor just said?' her husband gently scolded her. 'We have to follow his orders. You'll just have to get used to the idea of being the one who needs looking after,' he added with an attempt at humor.

'That's right,' Bruce McGregor confirmed. 'Actually,' he added, 'I've decided that perhaps there are too many visitors here at the moment. One at a time would be a better arrangement. You need to rest.' He smiled to soften his words.

'Does that mean we have to leave?' Dani asked.

'For now. But you can come back later,' the doctor suggested.

'Is it all right if I stay for a while?' Reginald asked.

'Of course' came the reply. 'Just make sure you don't overtire your wife.'

'I won't, I promise,' Reginald said with a loving glance at his wife. 'Go on home, Claire,' he said. 'I'll give you a call later, and you can come and pick me up.'

'Fine,' Claire said as she crossed to kiss her mother goodbye.

'Me, too,' Dani said, tugging at Claire's shorts. Claire lifted Dani to allow her to reach her grandmother.

'We'll be back later,' Claire told her mother as she followed Dr. McGregor from the room.

'She is going to be all right, isn't

she?' Claire asked the minute the door swung closed behind her.

'The attack was a mild one,' Dr. McGregor assured her. 'And thanks to Dani's prompt call, there were paramedics on the scene within a few minutes,' he said. 'But that doesn't mean we should ignore what happened.'

'*Dr. McGregor to the O.R., please. Dr. McGregor to the O.R.*' The disembodied voice of the hospital's PA system cut in.

'Sorry, Claire, I have to go,' Bruce said. 'I'll talk to you soon,' he added before hurrying off.

'Are we going home, now?' Dani asked as they retraced their way to the elevators.

'We may have to wait for Daniel,' Claire said.

'He's nice. I like him,' Dani announced, and at her words Claire felt a stab of guilt.

When they reached the parking lot there was no sign of Daniel. The temperature, already in the high seventies, was climbing steadily as the sun made its ascent into a cloudless blue sky.

Claire unlocked the car and stood undecided for a moment wondering whether to drive to Main Street and look for Daniel, or return to the hospital and wait in the comfort of the air-conditioned building.

'Here he is,' Dani said, pointing to the figure making his way between a row of parked cars.

Claire followed her daughter's gaze and felt her heart kick against her rib cage as she watched Daniel approach. He carried a shopping bag in one hand, and as well as the purchases in the bag, he'd bought himself a wide-brimmed hat as protection against the sun's damaging rays.

The hat reminded Claire of the one worn by Indiana Jones, that daring and handsome hero of several action-packed movies, and as Daniel came closer, she thought the resemblance between the two men even more striking.

Though Daniel's hair was black instead of dark brown, there was about him the same aura of self-confidence, strength of character and devil-may-care attitude that was part and parcel of the famous fictional hero. And while Indiana Jones had great sex appeal, Daniel somehow elevated that appeal to a new level. There was a dangerously potent masculinity about him that drew a response from somewhere deep within her.

'Hi. I like your hat,' Dani said with a friendly grin, when he reached the car.

Daniel flashed his daughter a heart-stopping smile, and Claire had to lick lips that were suddenly dry, hating herself for wishing the smile had been for her. Damn the man, she thought, as she reached for the mechanism that would unlock all the car doors.

'How's your mother?' Daniel asked as he opened the rear door and, after tossing his hat in, quickly followed.

'Tired, but all right,' Claire replied as

she started the engine and turned on the car's air-conditioning system.

'The doctor says she has to stay in the hospital for awhile,' Dani told him as she fastened her seat belt.

'I'm sorry to hear that,' Daniel said. 'You'll miss her.'

'Did you manage to find everything you needed?' Claire asked as she turned the car in the direction of home.

'Yes, thanks. The clerk at Spencer's — I believe she said her name was Debbie — was very helpful,' Daniel replied.

I bet! thought Claire, then frowned in annoyance to discover that the emotion chasing through her was jealousy. What was it about this man that affected her so deeply, arousing such strong and often conflicting emotions?

'I had no idea this part of the world was so picturesque,' Daniel commented as Claire brought the car to a halt at a traffic light.

'Rainbow Lake is my favorite place,' Dani said. 'It's the prettiest lake in the whole world,' she told him. 'Couldn't we . . . ' she began, glancing at her mother.

'Grandpa will need a ride home later, remember? We have to wait till he calls,' Claire said, and at her words Dani subsided into silence once more, her disappointment palpable.

'What is there to do at Rainbow Lake?' Daniel asked.

Dani immediately brightened. 'There's a neat playground with all kinds of things to climb on,' Dani explained eagerly. 'And you can swim in the lake 'cause it's roped off in the summertime and there's always a guard watching out for everybody.'

'Can you swim?' Daniel asked.

Dani nodded vigorously. 'Grandma says I swim like a fish,' she told him. 'Doesn't she, Mom?'

'She certainly does. And you most definitely do,' Claire replied, a hint of parental pride in her tone. Dani had been a water baby from a very early age and Claire had happily encouraged her daughter's penchant for swimming, enrolling her in lessons even before she was five.

'From as far back as I can remember, swimming has always been my favorite thing to do in the summer,' Daniel said.

'Really? Me, too,' Dani responded.

'My brother and I used to spend every summer at my grandparents' cottage on the shores of Lake Ontario,' Daniel said. 'We practically lived in the water,' he said, his voice softening at the memory.

'Lucky you,' Dani said. 'I wish we lived closer to Rainbow Lake,' she added with a sigh. 'Then I could go swimming every day, too.'

As Claire turned into the driveway, she found herself thinking that this was the first time she'd heard Daniel talk of his family. Not once during their time together in Italy had he ever brought up the subject; in fact, Claire recalled that every time she'd tried to ask him questions about himself, he'd answered evasively or simply smiled and changed the subject.

At the time she hadn't thought much about it. She'd respected his obvious wish for privacy. But later, when he'd failed to appear in Paris as he promised, she'd realized that he hadn't wanted her to know.

'Mom! Can I go next door and see if Taylor wants to play?' Dani asked as she hopped out of the car.

'All right,' Claire said, 'but come right back if she isn't home,' she added as she closed the driver door and started up the stairs.

'Okay!' Dani called as she scampered off across the lawn.

Claire unlocked the front door and, once inside, headed for the kitchen. She was hot and thirsty, and a drink of ice-cold water was first on her agenda. After filling a glass, she turned to find Daniel standing watching her, a look of determination in the depths of his gray eyes.

'I think it's time you answered a few questions. Don't you?' he said.

7

Claire lifted the glass of water to her lips and, taking a tiny mouthful, let the ice-cold liquid trickle down her parched throat.

'Fire away,' she said with a bravado she was far from feeling. She knew with a sense of inevitability that nothing and no one would deter him from his quest.

'When do you plan on telling Dani that I'm her father?' he challenged. 'I think we should tell her the truth as soon as possible . . . Right now, in fact. Unless, of course, you've painted a negative picture for her . . . '

'I've done no such thing,' Claire denied hotly.

'All right,' Daniel said calmly. 'What have you told her?' he asked, his steely gray eyes intent on hers.

Claire held his gaze defiantly. 'I told her I met her father on a beach in Italy when I was eighteen, and that the relationship didn't work out,' she said. She refrained from adding that she'd romanticized the events somewhat, before explaining as best she could to a child of such tender years, that at eighteen she'd been young and naive, not to mention foolish, to have pinned all her hopes and dreams on what had turned out to be nothing more than just another holiday romance.

'That was generous of you,' Daniel acknowledged, a hint of surprise in his tone. 'If that's the case, telling her the truth should be relatively easy, don't you agree?'

'I haven't really had time to think about it,' Claire replied, especially in view of all that had taken place in the past twenty-four hours. But if the truth be known, she didn't want to think about it, wanted to avoid the issue altogether.

'Perhaps it's time you did,' Daniel said with an edge to his voice that was fast becoming familiar.

Claire set the water glass on the kitchen table. 'It's too soon. I think we should wait,' she said. 'Dani's been through rather a lot . . . what with my mother's heart attack and having to call the ambulance . . . going to the hospital.' She ground to a halt knowing her argument was weak. 'She is only seven,' she quickly added, a hint of desperation in her tone. 'I don't think she's ready to cope with another bombshell at the moment. I suppose you'll think I'm being overprotective . . . ' Claire stopped once more and a shiver chased down her spine as she watched Daniel's gray eyes darken to a molten silver.

Her excuse was lame at best. Dani appeared to have suffered no after-effects from the trauma she'd gone through. She'd handled the situation like a trooper and, no doubt because of the positive outcome, she'd bounced back, a typical reaction of most young children.

'She doesn't need protection from

me,' Daniel stated coldly, obviously taking offense at her last remark.

Claire dropped her gaze and felt her cheeks grow warm under his continued scrutiny. She knew he was right, and in some private corner of her mind she also knew that *she* was the one who wasn't ready to face the consequences of telling Dani the truth, that the only person she was protecting was herself.

'Tell me,' Daniel continued in a controlled voice. 'Why didn't you get in touch with me when you found out you were pregnant?'

The question was like a slap in the face. Claire's head snapped up and she stared in stunned disbelief at Daniel. Seconds ago she'd been on the verge of weakening, of giving in to his demand that she tell Dani the truth, but his question only served to strengthen her resolve not to allow him to run roughshod over her.

Besides, how could he even ask the question, when he already knew the answer?

'You don't really expect me to answer that, do you?' Claire countered, startled to see the look of confusion that flashed in the depth of his eyes.

'Why not? It's straightforward enough,' Daniel replied, his features creased in a frown.

'All right, I'll play it your way,' Claire said, anger lacing her voice now. 'I didn't contact you because I had no idea where you lived. You didn't leave a forwarding address.'

Her words were met with complete and total silence. The air between them crackled with tension and Claire wondered fleetingly if Daniel had even heard what she said. He stood like a statue carved out of stone, staring blankly at her.

Suddenly the front door slammed shut and the sound of someone running across the tiled foyer cut through the silence, effectively capturing their attention. Seconds later, Dani, her eyes sparkling with excitement, came racing into the kitchen.

'Mom! Mom! Can I go swimming at Rainbow Lake with Taylor? Please? Can I?' she pleaded.

Claire frowned, knowing her daughter all too well and betting that Dani had coaxed Taylor into making the request. Taylor, a year younger than Dani, tended to let Dani be the leader when they played.

'Did you by any chance tell Taylor to ask her mother?' Claire inquired.

Dani blinked several times and, lowering her eyes, began to study her feet. 'I just said it was hot and it would be fun to go swimming at the lake,' she explained, her brown curls falling forward to hide her face.

'I know you want to go swimming, darling, but Grandpa will be calling soon to get a ride home, and as I said before, we can go to the lake another day,' Claire said.

'Aw, Mom,' Dani said, but before she could say more the sound of a car's tires on the gravel outside caught Claire's attention.

She turned and glanced out of the kitchen window in time to see Rick Robson, the man who worked in the real-estate offices next to Farmer's Antiques in town, climb out of the car.

'Is it Grandpa?' Dani asked, ever hopeful.

'No, it's not Grandpa. It's Mr. Robson,' she said.

'Mr. Robson? Oh, your boyfriend,' Dani said with a giggle as she flashed a grin at Daniel.

Claire swung around to glare at her daughter. 'Rick Robson isn't my boyfriend,' she denounced, aware all the while of Daniel's speculative glance.

'But you went out on a date with him,' Dani replied, unperturbed by her mother's denial.

'That's true,' Claire conceded as she moved around the table. 'But we're friends — that's all,' she said. 'Excuse me,' she added before heading off toward the front door to greet Rick.

Dani was right. A month ago she had gone out on a date with Rick. But that was after declining countless invitations to join him for dinner after work. Her mother had been the one who'd finally coaxed her into accepting, saying it was time she dated more, time she threw her hat into the ring, perhaps even time she fell in love again.

Claire had scoffed at the notion. Falling in love had brought her nothing but heartache and disillusionment. She'd learned her lesson well, and for the past eight years her life had been much too busy to even contemplate putting time and effort into a relationship. Not that there had been anyone she'd been remotely interested in.

Claire opened the front door as Rick came up the front steps.

'Hi, Claire,' Rick greeted her with a friendly smile. Thirty-five and divorced, he seemed anxious to find himself a new partner in life, but Claire wasn't altogether sure she wanted to be in the running for the job.

'Hello, Rick. What brings you here?' she asked.

'I heard about your mother. How is she?'

'She's doing well, thank you,' Claire replied. 'Come in,' she invited, opening the door wide. 'Can I offer you a cup of coffee?'

'Thanks, but I can't stay,' he said, stepping into the tiled foyer. 'Jerry Hamera, one of the night nurses, told me this morning when I saw her in the coffee shop. I'm so glad Dorothy's doing all right. I tried to call you, but there was no answer.'

'Reg wanted to get to the hospital,' Claire explained as she shut the front door. 'We drove in with him earlier, and he decided to stay and sit with my mother for a while.'

'I see,' Rick replied. 'I had to come out this way to meet a client,' he went on. 'I thought I'd drop by on my way and see if there was anything I can do.'

'Thank you, Rick,' Claire said, touched by his thoughtfulness.

'Oh, I'm sorry, I didn't know you had company,' Rick went on, catching sight of Daniel with Dani beside him, coming from the kitchen. 'Hi, Dani,' he added, smiling at the child.

'Hi,' Dani replied, her smile friendly.

'Rick, I'd like you to meet Daniel Hunter . . . He's . . . a friend . . . of the family,' she explained, stumbling over her words. 'Daniel, this is Rick Robson, a local real-estate agent.'

In three strides, Daniel, a polite smile on his face, crossed to shake Rick's outstretched hand.

Claire watched in fascination as the men eyed each other speculatively. Like two opponents sizing each other up in preparation for an upcoming bout, they seemed to be gauging and assessing, looking for strengths and weaknesses.

'Nice to meet you.' Both men spoke at the same time.

'How is the real-estate market in this area?' Daniel asked.

'Business is always active during the summer months,' Rick responded. 'Are you on the lookout for some property?' he asked, the consummate salesman eyeing a potential client.

'I'm a man who likes to find a bargain wherever I go,' Daniel replied easily. 'But that's almost impossible these days, especially when dealing with real estate,' he added.

'Wouldn't you agree?'

'Yes, I would,' Rick answered automatically. 'But it's funny you should mention a bargain,' he went on, a curious smile on his face. 'Because there is one property in the area that could prove to be one of the great bargains of the decade. For someone lucky enough to take advantage of an opportunity, of course,' he added with a laugh.

'Really?' Daniel said. 'Pray tell . . . '

'It's the Braeside estate,' Rick replied. 'The property itself is going up for auction at the end of the week, after the household contents are auctioned off.'

Daniel threw Claire a questioning glance and received a nod confirming that this was the same estate sale Reginald had suggested he see.

191

'The house itself could use a few repairs, but nothing a good carpenter couldn't handle quite easily,' Rick continued, obviously aware that he had an interested audience.

'And you think it will go for a reasonable price?' Daniel asked.

'Let me put it this way,' Rick replied, his smile widening. 'If there's someone who happens to have two hundred and fifty thousand dollars or so to spare, they could certainly get a darned good deal,' he concluded affably.

'How interesting,' Daniel said politely.

'Well, if you'll excuse me, I'd better be going. Don't want to be late meeting with a client,' he said. 'See you later, Dani.' He patted the child's head. 'It was nice to meet you,' he told Daniel, before turning to Claire once more. 'You will let me know if there's anything I can do?'

'Yes, and thanks for dropping by, Rick,' Claire said as she opened the door.

He hesitated in the doorway, taking

her hand in his. 'Maybe we can go for dinner again sometime,' he suggested.

Claire hesitated. While she did like Rick and had enjoyed their evening out together, accepting another invitation might send him the message that she was interested, when in fact she wasn't. Behind her, however, she sensed Daniel was also waiting to hear her answer.

'That would be lovely,' she responded, hoping in some perverse way to show Daniel that she wasn't still yearning for him, that her life was just fine. But seeing the light of hope flicker in Rick's eyes, she instantly regretted her words.

'Great. I'll call you,' Rick said before leaning over and kissing her gently on the cheek.

'Bye,' Claire said, managing a tight smile, and after closing the door, turned to see her daughter and Daniel staring at her. For a fleeting moment Claire saw a flash of an emotion she couldn't quite decipher flicker in Daniel's gray eyes before he quickly controlled it.

'Mommy . . . he kissed you,' Dani

said, her words effectively distracting Claire.

'I know,' Claire replied, exasperation rippling through her.

'Are you going to marry him? Is he going to be my new daddy?' Dani asked, her tone serious.

'No, I'm not going to marry him. I'm not going to marry anyone,' Claire was quick to reply. 'At least not any time soon,' she added, strictly for Daniel's benefit.

'Grandma thinks you should get married while you're still young,' Dani said. 'I heard her and Grandpa talking,' she added. 'How long will it be until you're too old?' Dani wanted to know.

Claire managed to curb the rumble of laughter suddenly threatening to erupt, but she lost the battle with the smile that curled at her mouth. She glanced at Daniel and felt her breath lock in her throat to see an answering smile tugging at his lips and the glint of humor dancing in his eyes.

'What's so funny?' Dani asked,

frowning at her mother.

'It's considered rude to make comments or ask questions about a woman's age,' Daniel explained, effectively distracting Dani.

'Why?' asked the child.

'Just wait until you're older, and you'll understand,' Claire told her evenly. 'But to answer your question, I'm not sure anyone is ever too old to get married.'

'But you have to be in love first. Right?' Dani asked, obviously enjoying the attention her questions were receiving.

This time, however, her words were met with an uncomfortable silence. The air seemed alive with tension, but before anyone spoke, the telephone rang.

Claire almost sighed aloud with relief as she quickly turned away from Daniel's probing gaze and crossed to where the telephone lay on an antique table at the foot of the stairs.

Daniel's eyes lingered on Claire for a

moment. While it had been eight years since he'd last seen her, the changes he noticed were both subtle and alluring. There was a quiet maturity about her, an assuredness that had undoubtedly evolved through her own personal growth. He let his gaze drift over her, noting the lightly tanned but decidedly slender legs, her firm round buttocks and slim waistline, widening to full-figured roundness.

All at once the memory of Claire's naked body moving seductively beneath his besieged him, and the sudden sharp stab of desire that accompanied the memory rocked him to the core.

Aware that Dani was studying him, Daniel slowly released the breath he hadn't known he'd been holding and began to retrace his steps to the kitchen.

'Want some juice?' he asked as he opened the fridge. He needed something cool and bracing himself, cold enough to chase away the gnawing ache spreading through him, an ache he hadn't felt in quite some time.

'Yes, please,' Dani replied, and Daniel swiftly complied, setting a glass of juice on the kitchen table before sitting down opposite his daughter.

'Do you think my mom's pretty?' Dani asked.

Daniel almost choked on the mouthful he'd just taken. 'Yes,' he answered truthfully.

'Do you think Mr. Robson likes her?' Dani continued.

'Oh . . . yes,' he replied trying to keep the sarcasm out of his voice. That Rick Robson liked Claire a great deal had been patently obvious, Daniel thought, surprised by the stab of irritation this thought evoked.

'Then maybe he will be my new daddy one day,' Dani said, and at his daughter's words, Daniel felt a sudden and almost overwhelming urge to trample Rick Robson into the ground.

'Do you like him?' Daniel asked, curious to learn just what his daughter thought of the other man.

'He's okay, I suppose,' Dani answered matter-of-factly.

'Tell me. What do you think a dad should be like?' Daniel asked, intrigued to hear how she would respond.

Dani sipped juice from her glass, her expression thoughtful. 'Dads should play with their kids all the time and never get mad at them. And dads should teach their kids neat things, like how to ride a two-wheeler, how to play checkers, how to wrestle or maybe even how to dive . . . That'd be super 'cause I want to learn how to dive,' she ended in a rush.

'You do?' Daniel said.

'Yes, but Mom doesn't know how and Grandma and Grandpa can't 'cause they're too old. There's no one who'll teach me.' Dani stopped and set the glass down. 'Do you know how to dive?' she asked.

'Yes,' Daniel said, thinking all the while that he'd happily teach her everything on her list.

'Wow . . . could you teach me?' she

ventured to ask, her gray eyes so like his own glowing with barely suppressed excitement as she waited for his answer.

'I'd love to,' Daniel said and was rewarded by the brightest and most beautiful smile he'd ever seen. He felt his heart expand with love, and not for the first time he wished he could take her in his arms and squeeze her tight.

Claire appeared behind Dani and Daniel glanced up at her, noticing the frown. 'Something wrong?' he asked.

'No,' said Claire. 'That was Reginald on the phone.'

'Are we going to get Grandpa now?' Dani asked, twisting around to look at her mother.

'No, Grandpa said he's going over to the store for awhile and we can pick him up at the hospital around four,' she reported.

'If we're not picking up Grandpa now, can we go to Rainbow Lake instead?' Dani was quick to ask. 'We could take a picnic and go for a swim. *He* said he would teach me how to dive,' Dani announced, pointing at her father. 'Can we go? Please?' Dani pleaded.

Claire's heart took a strange leap as she glanced from father to daughter. It was easy to see the family resemblance between them, especially when their expressions were almost identical. Daniel's dark eyebrows were arched in silent query while Dani's forehead crinkled in exactly the same way as her father's.

Much as she wanted to, she couldn't think of a valid objection to the outing; in fact, Claire decided that it might be a good opportunity to see how Daniel interacted with Dani. Perhaps they wouldn't get along. Trying to teach a seven-year-old anything, let alone how to dive, might prove more challenging than he realized.

'All right,' Claire said, 'but I better call Taylor's mom and explain what's happening.'

Dani whooped with delight and Claire couldn't quite stop the smile that curved at her mouth in response to her daughter's enthusiastic outburst.

'Go find your bathing suit and put it on. I'll make a few sandwiches and put together a picnic basket,' Claire said. 'Oh . . . ' An alarming thought just entered her head. She turned to Daniel. 'You do have a bathing suit, don't you?' she asked, and felt the blood rush to her cheeks when once again she saw the flash of humor in his eyes, telling her clearly that he, too, was recalling the circumstance of their initial meeting eight years ago.

'I never leave home without one,' Daniel replied easily. 'I did once,' he went on, a devilish gleam in his eyes now, a gleam that sent Claire's blood pressure soaring. 'And it led to a bundle of trouble,' he concluded, his eyes shifting to Dani.

'I'll show you where Mom keeps the picnic blanket. And we'll need towels, too, right, Mom?' Dani said, oblivious to the interplay going on between the two adults.

'Good idea,' Claire said, glad of Dani's chatter which helped defuse the tension simmering in the air. 'Don't forget to bring your sun hat,' she added before turning her back on Daniel and crossing to the large storage cupboard where she knew she would find the old wicker picnic basket.

Half an hour later Claire put the picnic basket in the trunk of the car and climbed behind the wheel. Dani opted for the back seat while Daniel slid into the passenger seat beside her.

To Daniel's surprise Dani was silent as Claire drove along the colorful country roads. Claire, too, seemed disinclined to chat, and Daniel found his thoughts returning to her stunning reply to his question earlier.

He *had* left her his address. He'd written it on the note he left at her hotel in Paris. He'd even had the taxi driver make a detour on the way to the airport, so that he could give the envelope to the desk clerk, himself.

In the letter he'd explained about the

call he'd had from home telling him his father had been badly injured in a car accident and that he'd had to fly home. He'd printed his address and phone number on the note and asked her to contact him as soon as she arrived in Paris. He'd calculated that by the time the tour bus reached the hotel, he'd already be in Boston.

When he'd arrived home, his brother, Paul, had met him with the news that their father was in critical condition and that Thomas Albright, a close friend and business associate of his father's, had died in the car crash.

For the next forty-eight hours Daniel had remained at his father's bedside, keeping a vigil, along with his mother and brother. Not until the doctors assured him his father was out of danger and on the road to recovery had Daniel's thoughts turned to Claire. He'd returned home, expecting to at least find a message from her, but apart from some messages from concerned family friends, no one had called from Paris.

That's when he'd placed a call to the hotel in Paris himself, in the faint hope of catching her there. But his frustration had doubled when the clerk had been unable to locate anyone named Claire MacInnes.

A week later when he still hadn't heard from her, he'd put in a call to the University of Toronto, but again he'd come up empty-handed, and while he knew Claire had grown up in the province of British Columbia, he hadn't had a clue where to start looking for her there.

And so the trail had petered out, leaving him to assume that she'd had a change of heart. But if he was to believe what she'd said, that she hadn't received his letter, then it warranted further investigation.

Still, he silently reasoned, if she'd come to Boston with Dani, she'd obviously remembered enough information about him to track him down. Why had she waited so long? Why hadn't she tracked him down when she discovered she was pregnant?

Daniel clamped down on the feelings of frustration and anger threatening to resurface. While he wanted to tackle Claire again on the issue of the note he'd sent her, Dani's presence made that impossible.

There was little he could do to change the past; what was important now was Dani, and he vowed that nothing and no one would stop him getting to know his daughter.

The thought of another man laying claim to his daughter did not sit well with him, either, but he was a patient man. And Claire's stubbornness on the issue of telling Dani the truth would, he felt sure, be resolved in time.

'We're here!' Dani announced from the back seat. 'Wow, the parking lot's really full,' she added. 'Oh, there's a spot. See!' she quickly pointed out.

'I see it,' Claire replied as she pulled into the narrow space.

'This looks like a popular place,'

Daniel commented as he opened the passenger door and got out.

A few minutes later, Claire, with a blanket and towels over her arm, led Daniel, carrying the picnic basket, to the path leading to the picnic and swimming areas. The hot summer temperatures had obviously prompted vacationers and locals alike to spend the day on the shores of the lake.

While Dani ran ahead to scout for a location in the shade, yet near enough to the lake, Claire, wearing a wide-brimmed straw hat, felt the perspiration break out on her forehead as she tried to keep up with her daughter.

'Over here!' Dani called and Claire quickly adjusted her stride, taking the path to the right to where Dani stood under a shady silver birch tree.

'This is great!' Daniel said as he set the basket on the ground. Pushing back the brim of his hat, he took off his sunglasses and studied the land-scape. The sandy area on the lakeshore was scattered with suntanned bodies stretched out on towels and blankets or hiding under umbrellas for protection from the sun's powerful rays.

The water looked cool and inviting and a tree-covered hillside rose up from the opposite side of the lake. Daniel noticed a variety of cabins, each with its own boat and pier, strategically placed around the lake. The view itself was spectacular.

The noise of children playing, the strains of music from ghetto blasters and the hum of motorboats farther out on the lake filled the air. Near the shore the area used for public swimming had been cordoned off by large orange buoys. A lifeguard's chair had been set up in the shallow water, allowing the guard a bird's-eye view of the swimmers and the small diving platform off the pier.

The blue-green water was dotted with bodies bobbing and splashing and Daniel could smell smoke from grills as picnickers barbecued nearby in designated spots. Beside him, Dani was already removing her shorts and T-shirt to reveal a snazzy pink-and-purple swimsuit.

'Coming?' she asked Daniel.

'Wait! First give me a hand to spread out the blanket,' Claire instructed. 'Then I'll rub some waterproof sunscreen on before you go in the water.'

'Here, let me,' Daniel said, taking the blanket from Claire.

'Do you want Mom to put sunscreen on your back, too?' Dani asked her father several minutes later when Claire had finished anointing Dani's back and shoulders.

'Sure,' Daniel replied, dropping down onto the blanket beside them and shrugging off his shirt.

Claire felt her mouth go dry and her heart shudder to a halt as she stared at his bronzed and muscled back. Eight years simply fell away and she suddenly found herself transported back to the beach in Camiore when she'd lovingly explored the hard contours of his body, those broad shoulders and wide chest, tapering down to a flat stomach and smooth hips.

'Have you run out of lotion?' Daniel asked, glancing at her over his shoulder, his dark eyebrows arching in puzzlement.

'No . . . ' Claire squeaked, dragging her thoughts away from the past. She coughed to hide her distress and wished she could simply refuse to comply. But with Dani glaring at her impatiently, she had no choice.

With the tips of her fingers, she gently smoothed the lotion across his shoulders and down his back, stopping at the waistband of his shorts. His body was as lean and fit as it had been eight years ago and as she slowly stroked her hands over his warm, firm flesh, a familiar heat began to spiral through her veins.

Her lungs seemed to be suddenly laboring under the effort and her pulse was skipping crazily as she fought to ignore the aching need spreading insidiously through her. It took every ounce of willpower not to press her lips against the strong column of his neck, just as she'd done in similar circumstances eight years ago.

'There,' Claire said, her voice husky with emotion. With trembling fingers she replaced the cap on the bottle of sunscreen.

'Thanks,' Daniel said, his tone gruff as he got to his feet.

Claire kept her eyes averted as he undid the snap on his shorts and pulled down the zipper. The sound made her uneasy, and she turned away to the picnic basket, unable to watch as he removed his shorts.

'Are you going to swim, too, Mom?' Dani asked.

'I didn't bring my bathing suit,' she said, having deliberately forgotten to pack the item. 'I'll just watch from here,' Claire said, her nerves jangling, her emotions in chaos.

'Okay,' Dani said.

Daniel tossed his sunglasses onto the blanket. 'Race you to the water!' he challenged, but almost before he'd finished speaking, Dani took off like a bullet from a gun, leaving Daniel laughing and shaking his head.

Claire watched as Daniel, wearing a black bathing suit that accentuated his powerful thighs and firm buttocks, followed Dani down to the water's edge. That he was one of the most magnificent specimens of masculinity she'd ever seen was made doubly obvious by the admiring glances thrown his way by almost every woman within a radius of a hundred feet.

Her fingers still tingled from the contact with him and every cell hummed with remembered excitement. Muttering under her breath, Claire reached into the basket to extract an ice-cold bottle of mineral water, hoping somehow to take the edge off the need tugging insistently at her insides.

For the next hour Claire watched from her vantage point as Daniel patiently and painstakingly taught Dani how to dive. Try after try, he gently coached and corrected his eager pupil. Always with a smile and always encouraging her, even taking time out to simply splash and play when Dani became too frustrated with her efforts.

At the end of the hour, however, Dani was showing marked improvement until at last she succeeded in mastering a perfect dive. Her yell of joy as she broke the water's surface could have been heard for miles. Claire smiled and waved to acknowledge that she'd indeed been watching.

A few minutes later, a tired but exhilarated Dani came running back to the blanket, flopping down onto her waiting towel.

'Did you see me dive?' she demanded excitedly, her eyes wide, her smile full of confidence.

'Yes, I saw you,' Claire replied. 'Well-done. You were terrific,' she added.

'I'm starved,' Dani said.

'Me, too,' Daniel said as he reached the blanket. 'Thanks,' he said as Claire handed him a towel.

Claire served up the sandwiches and chips and cold drinks, and Dani lay on her stomach watching the swimmers as she munched on her picnic lunch.

After towel drying his hair, Daniel sat down on the towel, surprised at how tired he felt, but surprised, too, at just how much fun he'd had with Dani. That she'd been a willing pupil was obvious by the way she'd listened and tried to do as he suggested. Determination was a trait his daughter had inherited from his side of the family — of that he was sure — and the joy that had filled him when she'd dived cleanly into the water had been surpassed only by the overwhelming feeling of love he'd experienced when she'd thrown her arms around him, purely and simply out of utter and uncontainable delight at succeeding.

He wasn't sure he'd ever be able to forget the feeling of holding her in his arms; he only knew that those brief but precious moments would remain imprinted on his heart forever.

'Want to go swimming again?' Dani asked her father as soon as they'd finished the cookies Claire had brought for dessert.

'Dani, maybe you should have a break for a while,' Claire suggested. 'Aren't you tired from all that diving? I am, just from watching you,' she added teasingly.

'I'm not tired,' Dani declared.

'Me, either,' Daniel said, as he rose to his feet.

'I thought it wasn't a good idea to swim right after you've eaten,' Claire said.

'That's an old wives' tale,' Daniel said. 'But maybe we shouldn't try diving, but play in the shallow area for a while,' he suggested.

'We could play catch,' Dani said.

'Great! Let's go!' Daniel said, and Claire could only shake her head as she watched them make their way back to the water.

After tidying away the remnants of their picnic, Claire stretched out on the

214

blanket and closed her eyes. Throughout the meal she'd been all too aware of
Daniel's nearly naked body lying a few
inches away. If she'd reached out, she
could have touched him, ran her fingers
down the length of his torso, as she'd
done so many times before during those
magical days so long ago.

The desire to know again the heady
rush of excitement when his hand
captured hers before making a foray of
its own, teasing, tantalizing and igniting
a fire that scorched a path to every
nerve and every cell, had been almost
more than she could resist.

With a sigh of frustration she drifted
into a fitful sleep as memories she'd just
as soon forget, danced inside her head.

* * *

'Claire. Claire.'

Daniel's deeply seductive voice calling her name brought a smile to her
lips. She had been dreaming about him.
She stretched languidly and opened her

eyes, instantly seeing Daniel's handsome face and those incredible gray eyes only a few inches away, glinting with amusement at her.

'Hey, sleepyhead! Don't look at me like that,' Daniel cautioned softly, his words sending a shiver of longing spiraling through her. She reached out, intending to pull him closer, powered by a need to feel his body against hers and to watch his eyes darken with passion.

A child's cry suddenly penetrated her hazy thoughts and as her surroundings came into sharp focus, she realized with a start that they weren't alone on the secluded beach at Camiore — they weren't even in Italy.

Shock and embarrassment mingled to bring a gasp of horror to her lips. Abruptly she sat up, wishing a hole would simply open up and swallow her. It wasn't fair that even after all this time he still had the power to affect her so profoundly.

'Where's Dani?' she demanded, pulling as far away from him as she could.

'A young boy named Mark Alexander came over to join us in the water and I left them playing Frisbee together,' he quickly explained. 'They're near the lifeguard's chair,' he told her when she swung around to look for Dani.

'I must have fallen asleep,' Claire said, tension still skimming through her. Nervously she glanced at her watch. 'We should be going,' she said as she got to her feet. 'I'll go and tell Dani,' she added, anxious to put some distance between herself and Daniel.

She'd almost made a colossal fool of herself, she angrily chided herself, as she hurried down the slope to the water's edge. What on earth must he have thought seeing her reaching out to him like that, practically begging him to kiss her? Pain stabbed at her heart and she blinked away the tears suddenly stinging her eyes.

'Dani! It's time to go. We have to pick up Grandpa,' Claire said once she'd managed to attract her daughter's attention.

'See you, Mark,' Dani said, waving to her friend, before reluctantly joining Claire on the shore.

'Could we come back tomorrow?' Dani asked, after they'd gathered everything and began making their way back to the car.

'We'll see,' Claire replied, not at all sure she was ready to spend another afternoon with Daniel. Not if she had to fight those old painful memories, memories she'd just as soon forget.

'Mark wanted me to ask if you'd teach him to dive, too,' Dani said to her father as Claire backed out of the parking spot. 'But I told him I didn't know how long you'd be staying,' she continued.

'I'll be here until after the estate sale,' Daniel replied. 'Perhaps we can go to the lake again later in the week,' he added.

'That'd be great,' Dani responded. 'Oh, and Mark said your name and my name are almost the same. 'Cause your name's Daniel and mine is Dani. But that's short for Danielle, which is like Daniel,' she rambled, ending with a self-conscious giggle.

'You're absolutely right. Our names are almost the same,' Daniel commented evenly, throwing Claire a wide-eyed glance, suggesting with one compelling look that she'd just been handed a golden opportunity, perhaps the perfect opportunity, to tell Dani the truth.

8

Claire kept her eyes on the road ahead, choosing to ignore the opening being offered. Not yet! I'm not ready! She wanted to scream the words aloud but bit down on her lip to stop them from escaping.

She could tell by the tension emanating from the man beside her that Daniel was angry. Desperately she clung to the belief that she was doing what was best for Dani, mentally brushing aside the tiny voice inside her head telling her she was a coward.

Dani continued to chatter throughout the journey back to town. Periodically, Daniel would comment or answer a question, but Claire managed to tune them out, all the while wondering just how she would make it through the rest of the week. She knew she couldn't avoid the issue forever.

Dani had to be told. But not yet!

For the second time that day Claire pulled the car into the hospital parking lot and quickly found an empty space. As they walked together toward the doors, Claire couldn't help thinking that to any passerby they must look like a typical family: husband, wife and child.

She was surprised at the sharp pang of regret this thought evoked. They could have been a real family. Daniel had been the one who'd destroyed that dream when he'd broken his promise to meet her in Paris.

And now, just because he'd learned he was the father of her child, he expected to simply walk right back into her life and change all the rules.

While she acknowledged that as Dani's father he did have certain rights, she had rights, too. And she had no intention of letting him take control, not without a fight. She'd been managing her life just fine up until now, and she was perfectly happy she told herself resolutely, ignoring that annoying inner voice telling her she was lying to herself.

Daniel's presence was a threat, a threat she wasn't sure how to handle. That his interest lay solely with Dani was abundantly clear. Perhaps even now he was planning some strategy. He was a rich man and could afford the best lawyers.

A feeling of panic assailed her and all at once the thought of shipping Dani to Boston to visit her father for weeks or months at a time sent a pain searing through her. It wasn't going to happen. She wouldn't allow it.

She had to admit, however, that after watching Daniel teach Dani how to dive, a bond of friendship and trust had been forged between them. That he'd make a wonderful father was patently obvious, but she found herself wondering if Dani was simply a substitute for the child he'd lost so tragically.

'Mommy, there's Grandpa waving to us,' Dani said, pointing through the glass doors to the man standing inside.

'Hello there. Looks like you've been swimming,' Reginald said when they caught up to him.

'We did go swimming and I can dive now, Grandpa,' Dani was quick to announce. 'We had a picnic at Rainbow Lake and Daniel teached me how to dive,' she explained proudly.

'That's wonderful. Good for you,' Reginald said, smiling down at the child. 'Did you have a good time?' He directed his question at Daniel.

'I did indeed,' Daniel replied with sincerity.

'Have you been up to see Dorothy?' Claire asked, wondering how her mother was feeling.

'Yes,' Reginald said. 'I walked over from the store half an hour ago and went right up to her room. She says they did all kinds of tests on her. But she's looking a little better. She wanted to take a nap and I was so hot and thirsty from walking over here that I thought I'd come down to the cafeteria and get myself a cold drink. Want to join me?' he asked.

'Yes, please,' Dani promptly replied. 'Can I have some soda?' she asked, glancing at her mother for approval.

'All right,' Claire said. 'I'll slip upstairs and sit with Grandma for a little while,' she said as she punched the button for the elevator. 'I'll meet you in the cafeteria,' she added as the elevator door slid open.

Claire tapped lightly on the door to her mother's room before peeking around the door to see if she was awake.

'Claire, darling, come in. I was hoping you'd stop by before going home,' her mother said.

'Reg said you were napping. I just thought I'd peek in and sit with you,' Claire said as she crossed to the bed. 'How are you feeling?' she asked once she'd kissed her mother's pale cheek.

'A little better,' her mother replied. 'Though I don't seem to have much energy and I get tired rather easily,' she added with a sigh.

Feelings of guilt tugged at Claire. 'I promise I won't stay too long and overtire you,' she said.

'Don't be silly, darling. It's lovely to see you. But I can't help feeling that I'm letting you down,' Dorothy went on, her voice wavering slightly as tears filled her eyes.

'Mother, please. I'm the one who's let you down,' Claire said, handing her mother a tissue from the box on the bedside table. 'I know what a handful Dani can be, and I should have realized that looking after her was taking a toll on you. I've been taking you for granted and it was selfish of me to expect you to look after Dani all the time.'

'But I love the child. And I love looking after her,' Dorothy said, dabbing the moisture from her eyes.

'I know you do, and believe me, she loves you, too,' Claire was quick to assure her. 'But her welfare is my responsibility, not yours,' she declared.

'You need to look after yourself. That's why I'm going to make other arrangements for Dani when school starts.'

'Are you sure?' Dorothy asked, though Claire noted the look of relief that flashed briefly in her mother's eyes, telling her all too clearly that she had indeed been finding looking after Dani something of a strain.

'I'm very sure,' Claire said. 'Besides, that way you and Reginald can have more time together.'

'Speaking of Reginald,' said her mother, changing the topic. 'He told me all about Daniel Hunter.' She paused for a moment before continuing. 'He is the same Daniel, isn't he . . . ?' she asked. 'I mean . . . he is the man you met in Europe? He is Dani's father?'

Claire drew a steadying breath. 'Yes. He's Dani's father,' she answered.

'I thought he must be,' Dorothy said. 'That's why he's here, isn't it? Because he knows about Dani?'

'Yes,' Claire acknowledged with a sigh.

'Reginald wondered why I was asking so many questions about Daniel, so I told him . . . I had to,' her mother went on, giving Claire a guilty glance. 'I'm sorry, darling, but I just felt that under the circumstances he had a right to know.'

'Don't apologize, Mother. You did the right thing,' Claire said softly. 'And anyway, from the way Daniel is talking, the fact that he's Dani's real father won't be a secret for much longer.'

'Why do you say that? What's he doing to do? Does Dani know he's her father?' The questions came fast and furious and Claire could see that this new development was causing her mother some added anxiety.

'Mom, please,' Claire cautioned. 'You mustn't get worked up about this.' She clasped her mother's hands in hers and gave them a squeeze. 'I don't know what he's planning to do. And no, I haven't told Dani who he really is.'

Dorothy's eyes clouded with renewed distress. 'But, Claire . . . don't you think you should tell the child? Surely honest is the best policy. What does he . . . Daniel think?' she asked.

'He thinks I should tell her, but I disagree,' Claire said firmly, wishing her mother had taken her side.

'Are you sure that's the right choice, darling?' her mother asked. 'I know I've never met Daniel, but Reginald certainly has a high regard for the man. Dani's an intelligent child, mature for her age and old enough to deal with the truth. The longer you wait to tell her, the harder it will be,' she concluded.

Claire managed a weak smile. 'I'll tell her when the time is right,' she said gently. 'Besides, I didn't come in here to burden you with my troubles. You've got enough on your plate without worrying about me. What's the latest from Dr. McGregor?' she asked, directing the conversation away from the topic of Dani and her father.

'They did a barrage of tests. But I don't know when the results will be back,' her mother replied. 'Dr. McGregor came by earlier and said he'd know more in a day or two.'

'I think I'd better go and let you rest for a while. Reginald will probably drive in to see you later this evening. Dani and I will come by tomorrow,' Claire said.

'All right, dear,' her mother replied. 'But promise me you'll think about telling the child.'

'I promise,' Claire said.

Kissing her mother once more, Claire left the room and made her way to the cafeteria.

'She looks better, don't you think?' Reginald asked the moment Claire joined them at the table by the window overlooking the hospital's courtyard and rose garden.

'Yes, she does,' Claire agreed, though she wasn't altogether sure it was true. Her mother had looked pale and her concern about the appearance of Dani's father had obviously affected her a great deal. But until she herself knew

Daniel's intentions, there was little she could do to alleviate her mother's worry.

Throughout the journey home the two men chatted amicably in the back seat while Dani seemed content to gaze out at the passing scenery. Claire turned her thoughts to the problem of finding someone to look after Dani.

The fact that the summer months happened to be one of their busiest times of the year due to vacationers dropping into the antique store to browse and quite often buy only compounded the problem. As a temporary solution, Claire knew she could take Dani with her to the store. But the question remained what would she do in September once school started.

'Mom, I see Taylor outside in her yard,' Dani said as Claire brought the car to a halt in the driveway. 'Can I go over and play for a while?' she asked as she unbuckled her seat belt.

'All right,' Claire said. 'Supper will be ready in an hour,' she added as Dani scampered off across the lawn.

'Would you mind if I used your office and made a few calls?' Daniel asked as he carried in the picnic basket and blanket and set them on the kitchen table.

'Not at all,' Reginald replied. 'My office is at your disposal.'

'Thanks,' Daniel said before making his way from the room.

'If you don't mind, my dear,' Reginald said turning to Claire, 'I have a bit of a headache. I think I'll go and lie down for a while.'

'Good idea,' Claire said, noting the lines of strain and worry on her stepfather's features.

Feeling a little hot and sticky herself, Claire ran upstairs to her bedroom and indulged in a quick shower. Refreshed, she dressed in a cotton print skirt and pink blouse, before brushing her hair and applying a touch of color to her lips.

Back in the kitchen, she put on one of her mother's aprons and began to prepare supper. Taking four pieces of fresh corn on the cob she placed them on the draining board next to the sink.

'Need a hand?' The question startled her and she turned to see Daniel, his hair still wet from the shower, looking refreshed and irresistibly handsome in a pair of khaki pants and a matching shirt.

'I . . . well.' Claire felt her face grow warm as she tried to ignore the leap her heart took at the sight of him.

'Salads are my speciality, remember?' he said as he came around the table to stand beside her.

Claire drew a steadying breath, trying to suppress the shivers of awareness zipping up her spine. He was, of course, referring to the time they'd spent together in Italy when he'd prepared a delicious salad for their lunch each day. But she refused to react, refused to acknowledge that she hadn't forgotten those carefree days when she'd lost her heart to him.

'You'll find everything you need for a

green salad in the fridge,' she said, keeping her tone even.

'And where would I find a bowl?' he asked, taking a step closer.

Her heart somersaulted inside her breast and her pulse began to beat erratically as he brushed past her to open the fridge door. A scent, enticingly male and excitingly sensual, tickled her nostrils, arousing her senses and awakening needs she'd thought she'd buried in the darkest corner of her heart.

'I'll get you one,' she told him, surprised that her voice sounded normal. Moving away, she retrieved a salad bowl from the cupboard next to the stove.

'What's for dinner?' he asked as he removed a head of lettuce, two tomatoes, a bunch of green onions and some celery stalks from the fridge and set them on the cutting board on the opposite side of the sink.

'Barbecued chicken, corn on the cob and green salad,' Claire replied.

'Sounds great. Is the barbecue a gas

one? Or do you want me to get the charcoal started?' he asked.

'It's a gas one, and it's outside on the patio,' she told him as she placed the salad bowl on the counter in front of him.

'Thanks,' he said. 'Oh, by the way, while I have the chance, I'd like to set the record straight.'

'About what?' she asked as she casually picked up a piece of corn and began to remove the outer leaves.

'I did leave you a note with my address in Boston,' he said.

Claire swung around to meet his gaze. 'Really,' she retorted, more than a hint of sarcasm in her voice.

'Yes,' Daniel answered. 'I left it with the clerk at the front desk of your hotel,' he went on.

'If that's true, why didn't I get it?' she asked, faintly irritated by what she perceived as his unspoken accusation that she was lying.

'You tell me,' he challenged softly, as he tore the lettuce leaves and dropped them into the bowl.

Anger rippled through her, effectively erasing the disturbingly emotions his nearness had evoked a few moments ago. 'I didn't get your note, because you didn't write one,' she told him.

'Are you implying that I'm lying?' Daniel asked, his tone decidedly chilling.

Claire ignored the question. 'I just wish you'd been honest with me from the beginning instead of making promises you didn't intend to keep,' she retorted, her anger fueled by the icy glint she could see in the depths of his gray eyes.

'I was there . . . ' he began.

'I never saw you,' she rudely retorted, recalling all too well the pain and disappointment she'd felt when he hadn't shown up at their appointed meeting place in Paris. 'But then you had me fooled from the start,' she went on, anger in every syllable. 'I guess I was stupid and naive to think I could be anything more than a temporary diversion for a man like you.'

At her outburst, Claire saw Daniel's jaw tighten. 'If you don't believe me when I say I was in Paris, why should I believe you when you said you brought Dani to Boston?' he countered his voice controlled and void of emotion.

'Because I *was* there. Why would I lie?' Claire responded.

'Why would I?' he countered, his gaze steady on hers.

The silence stretched between them for several long seconds and Claire found it impossible to pull her eyes from Daniel's. Was he telling the truth? Could she believe him?

No. He had to be lying. She'd waited three long, lonely hours outside Notre Dame Cathedral before returning to the hotel. Hoping that perhaps he'd been delayed, she'd asked the desk clerk if there was a message for her. But he'd shaken his head and told her there were no messages . . . no letters. Each morning for the three days the tour had stayed in Paris before their return flight home, she'd asked the clerk the same question, only to be given the same answer.

Suddenly the sound of footsteps crossing the tiled hallway broke the spell that seemed to have wound itself around them. Claire spun away from Daniel and with renewed vigor tore the leaves from the corn.

'You two look rather industrious,' Reginald said as he joined them in the kitchen. 'Is there anything I could be doing?' he asked.

'You could light the barbecue,' Claire suggested. 'The chicken is on a platter in the fridge, all ready to go,' she told him.

'Right,' he replied. 'Daniel, can I offer you a glass of wine while you're working?' Reginald asked. 'We have a winery in the area, the Alexander Winery, owned and run by a friend of mine,' he went on. 'I highly recommend their Riesling or if you prefer red, their Cabernet Sauvignon is also an excellent wine.'

'I'd like to try the Cabernet if I may,' Daniel replied.

'Good choice,' Reginald said, crossing to the wine rack sitting atop the tiled counter and extracting a bottle from one of the shelves.

Half an hour later Dani scurried in just in time to wash her hands before sitting down to dinner. Throughout the meal the conversation was of a general nature and afterward Dani was assigned the task of helping to clear away the dishes and load the dishwasher.

'Want to play a game of croquet?' Dani asked once the kitchen had been tidied.

'I'd love to,' Daniel said eagerly. 'I used to play croquet with my grandfather and brother when I was a kid,' he added, a smile tugging playfully at his mouth. 'We always had lots of fun.' He grinned down at his daughter.

'Grandpa and me play it a lot and we're pretty good at it,' Dani said proudly.

'Sweetie, I don't feel much like

playing tonight,' Reginald said. 'Claire, why don't you take my place?'

'Mom, you can have the blue ball — that's the one Grandpa always uses,' Dani said. 'Mine is the red one and you can have the black one,' she told Daniel.

Claire was sorely tempted to say she didn't feel like playing, either, but felt sure that after her verbal exchange with Daniel in the kitchen, that he'd think she was deliberately trying to avoid him.

Outside, the wire hoops were already set up in the lawn and the game was soon underway. Dani started, of course, and Claire took her turn next, followed by Daniel.

'I'm winning! I'm winning!' Dani announced half an hour later as she knocked her ball through the second-to-last hoop.

Much to her daughter's amusement, Claire had muffed several shots along the way, and as a result had fallen to last place. She was determined, however, with this shot, to draw even with

Daniel, or perhaps pull into second place. Once again her efforts proved insufficient as she watched her blue ball roll across the grass to come to rest right next to Daniel's.

Dani instantly let out a whoop of excitement, clapping her hands together gleefully. 'You can beat Daniel now, Mom,' Dani said, jumping up and down.

Claire frowned. 'How?' she asked.

''Cause you get to hit the black one with your blue one, silly,' Dani pointed out, her grin wide.

Daniel, standing on the sidelines, was smiling, too.

'I don't understand,' Claire confessed, gazing in puzzlement at her daughter.

'It's what's called a 'croquet,'' Daniel explained, moving toward her. 'First you put your foot on the blue ball, then you hit it with your mallet and that should result in sending the black one, belonging to yours truly, in the opposite direction, or for that matter in whichever direction you like,' he concluded.

'Really,' Claire said, still not understanding. 'But, I still . . . '

'Allow me to demonstrate,' said Daniel, and before she could either move or protest, he shifted to stand behind her and, putting his arms around her, gently grasped hold of her hands in his.

Claire felt her heart jam against her rib cage in startled response as his body seemed to melt against hers, his thighs pressing seductively against her buttocks, his chest against her back and his chin resting comfortably on her shoulder.

His warm breath fanned her face, sending shivers of excitement racing through her, and Claire felt her pulse kick into overdrive. She closed her eyes in a vain attempt to shut out the overwhelming assault on her senses, but this action only served to heighten the sweet and incredibly erotic sensations that being held in his arms evoked.

'It's quite easy really,' Daniel said, his voice husky in her ear. 'You just do this,' he said, and bringing her arms together with his he swung the mallet and brought it down to make contact with the blue ball.

For a heart-stopping moment Claire thought she would faint from the wonder of having his arms around her once more. The rich masculine scent of him assailed her senses, drawing a response from deep inside. She'd forgotten how strong he was, how safe she felt enclosed in his embrace, and it was all she could do not to turn and offer her mouth for a kiss she knew would surely stir her soul.

'Claire. Telephone for you.' Reginald's voice drifted through the haze she was in, bringing her crashing back to earth.

'Coming,' she called, her voice vibrating with emotion. 'Carry on without me,' she said as she broke free of Daniel's embrace and hurried across the lawn to the house. But with each step that took her away from Daniel, she experienced a stab of pain somewhere in the region of her heart.

'I'm off to the hospital now,' Reginald said when she reached the house. 'I'll see you later.'

'Give Mother my love,' Claire told him as she crossed to pick up the receiver.

'Claire, it's Jane,' said the voice on the other end of the line.

'Jane, hello!' Claire was aware of her heart still beating wildly against her rib cage.

'I just called to ask about your mother,' Jane said. 'Reginald said she's going to be all right.'

'Yes, thank heavens,' Claire said with heartfelt emotion. 'The doctor wants her to stay in hospital till the end of the week, but he's assured us that she's going to be just fine,' she confirmed.

'I'm so relieved,' Jane responded, before launching into a discourse about a relative who'd suffered a far more damaging attack with less positive results.

Claire listened politely and made appropriate comments, but her thoughts were distracted by the memory of those devastating moments when she'd felt Daniel's body pressed evocatively against hers.

'Give your mother my best wishes,' Jane said, bringing Claire's attention back to her friend.

'I will,' Claire responded. 'It was sweet of you to call,' she added before replacing the receiver.

Claire turned and made her way to the living room window where, from her vantage point, she watched Daniel and his daughter play another game of croquet.

The sound of shared laughter, Daniel's deep and rich and sexy, joined by Dani's childish giggle, tugged strangely at her heart, and not for the first time she found herself wondering what would have happened had she contacted Daniel when she found out she was pregnant.

At first she'd been thrilled to learn that she was pregnant, that what they'd shared would live on in the child they'd made together. But slowly the realization that she would be solely responsible for the care and well-being of an infant filled her with fear. How could she look after a child and give it the love and attention every child deserved when she was little more than a child herself?

During those first few weeks after learning she was pregnant she'd fought a war with her conscience, which kept telling her that Daniel had a right to know about the baby growing inside her. But each time she thought about trying to track him down she'd quickly reminded herself that he'd been the one who'd chosen to walk away without as much as a goodbye.

The pain she'd experienced when she'd finally had to accept the fact that he wasn't going to appear, had been like nothing she'd ever known before. He'd been the one who'd had a change of heart, not her, and she'd be wise not to forget it.

Suddenly the sound of Dani's laughter broke through her wandering thoughts. At the sight of father and daughter making their way across the lawn toward the house, Claire quickly retreated to the kitchen.

'I beat Daniel two times,' Dani told her mother proudly as they entered the kitchen.

Pinning a smile on her face Claire turned to face them. 'Well-done,' she said, annoyed at the leap her pulse took as her gaze met Daniel's gray eyes. She quickly looked away. 'I think it's time you got ready for bed, darling,' Claire said, and instantly Dani's happy expression vanished.

'Do I have to?' she asked.

'Yes, you have to,' Claire answered. 'Do you want to have a bath now, or a shower in the morning?' she asked.

'A shower, please' came the prompt reply.

'All right. Go and get into your nightie, and don't forget to brush your teeth,' Claire said. 'I'll be up in a few minutes to read you a story.'

'I want Daniel to read me a story

tonight,' Dani announced, surprising both adults with her request.

Daniel flashed Claire a glance before responding. 'I'd love to read you a bedtime story,' he said, and Claire heard the faint rasp of emotion in his voice.

'Come on, let's go,' Dani said, and slipping her hand into Daniel's led him out of the kitchen.

Alone once more, Claire crossed to the fridge and poured herself a glass of ice tea. Opening the door leading onto the patio she wandered outside into the cool evening air, trying to understand the emotions churning inside her. Watching Dani walk off with Daniel, her small hand tucked trustingly inside his, had affected her more than she was willing to admit, as feelings of jealousy and something else, less easy to define, had sliced through her.

Her calm structured life was spinning out of control and there wasn't a thing she could do about it. Even Dani appeared to have taken Daniel's side and Claire couldn't help feeling that she, and not Daniel, was the one standing on the outside looking in.

She wasn't sure how long she stood staring across the valley spread before her like a giant colorful quilt. The evening sky had a pinkish glow that held the promise of another sunny day.

Since moving to Peachville when her mother married Reginald, Claire had grown to love the area, glad that Dani was spending her childhood years in a small-town community. Reginald's friends and the majority of folks living in and around Peachville had welcomed Claire and her mother and Dani, too, with open arms.

'She's asleep.' Daniel's voice came from behind her, and Claire spun around in surprise, almost dropping the empty glass cradled in her hand. 'Sorry, I didn't mean to startle you,' he went on.

'It's all right,' Claire replied. 'I was miles away,' she said.

'Dani's something special, isn't she?'

Daniel said, a smile curling at his mouth, his tone steeped in warmth and love.

'Yes, she is,' Claire said softly, wishing in some corner of her heart that he'd been talking about her and not Dani. Annoyance rippled through her at this thought, and not for the first time she wondered what there was about this man that affected her so deeply.

'Would you tell me about her?' Daniel asked. 'I mean, was she a good baby, did she cry a lot, what was her favorite toy?'

At these words Claire felt her annoyance melt away, replaced by an another emotion that disturbed her in an entirely different way. That he sincerely wanted to know about Dani was evident by the huskiness of his voice and the look of longing she could see shimmering in the silvery depths of his eyes.

Moved more than she cared to admit, Claire drew a ragged breath. 'She was a happy and contented baby,' she began. 'She rarely fussed and when she cried she usually had a good reason, like a dirty diaper, or because she was hungry. I could go and get the photo albums . . . ' she said.

'Thank you. I'd like that,' Daniel said.

'I'll be right back,' Claire said as she headed inside.

Claire returned to the kitchen bringing with her several albums full of photographs she'd taken of Dani since her arrival into the world on a beautiful May morning over seven years ago.

Daniel was in the kitchen when she returned and she set the books on the table and for the hour that followed Claire answered questions and made comments as she related stories about their daughter. Daniel couldn't seem to get enough as he flipped the pages back and forth, poring over the pictures, laughing at some of the candid shots Claire had taken, one in particular of Dani at the age of four, sitting on an antique rocking horse, her eyes sparkling with joy.

Claire couldn't help noticing that Daniel lingered over the earlier pictures, the ones of Dani as a newborn. He looked misty-eyed and thoughtful, sadness and pain simmering beneath the surface, making Claire think that he was recalling the short time he'd had with his son, Kevin.

They were still browsing through the albums when Reginald returned from the hospital. He stopped in briefly to say Dorothy sent her love, before wishing them both a pleasant goodnight.

'Claire, I want to thank you for sharing this with me,' Daniel said a little while later. 'I still can't believe that she's mine,' he added, leaning back in the chair and smiling at her. 'You've done a marvelous job. She's an incredible kid. It blows me away to think that together we created someone so beautiful.'

'Mmm,' Claire murmured, finding it

hard to get any words past the lump lodged in her throat.

'Perhaps you're right about not telling Dani I'm her father,' he said, and Claire blinked in surprise. 'At least, not until we've straightened things out between the two of us. Starting with the fact that I did leave you a note and in it I explained why I had to return to the States without seeing you,' he went on matter-of-factly. 'When I didn't hear from you, I assumed you'd had a change of heart.'

Claire said nothing. He sounded sincere, and while part of her wanted to believe that he'd had a valid reason for walking out of her life without as much as a by-your-leave, another, more cynical part of her, fed by the pain of his abandonment, a pain that ran too deeply, was already dismissing his claim.

'If anyone had a change of heart, it was you,' she challenged. 'And anyway, aren't you forgetting something? Your wedding to Kelly, the one I read about in the Boston paper on my flight back to Vancouver, had to have been planned for some time, and probably in the works when we met,' she concluded.

At her words, she saw Daniel's jaw tighten and a look of sadness came into his eyes.

'I can explain about Kelly,' he said with a sigh.

'I bet,' she countered. 'But I think I've heard enough lies,' Claire went on.

'Damn it, Claire, I'm not lying,' Daniel retorted, rising to his feet. 'What happened to the 'innocent until proven guilty' theory? What is it you're so afraid of, Claire?'

'Nothing!' she shot back angrily. 'The past is past. We can't go back, and no amount of explaining will change anything,' she told him, fighting back tears now.

'I suppose you're right,' he said, a sadness in his tone. 'But don't you think it would be better for everyone concerned to finally put the past to rest? That way we can all get on with the future.'

'I already have,' Claire replied, and with that she hurried from the kitchen.

In the sanctuary of her bedroom Claire let the tears flow. But she couldn't quite ignore the little voice inside her head telling her Daniel was right, that she was afraid. Afraid of having to face the possibility that she might have made the wrong decision when she'd decided not to tell Daniel about her pregnancy.

But at the back of her mind another thought surfaced, one that had crept into her mind all too often after Daniel walked out of her life, and one that had been the deciding factor against tracking him down.

Not once during those incredible four days in Camiore had Daniel told her how he felt about her, or what he felt for her. Not once had he ever spoken of love.

9

The next morning Claire was standing at the counter drinking coffee when her stepfather joined her in the kitchen.

'Good morning,' Reginald said, accepting the mug of coffee Claire handed him. 'I was just talking to Daniel upstairs a minute ago, and he's agreed to come into town with me this morning, to give me a hand in the store. The truck bringing the items from the Vancouver auction is due to arrive today,' he went on.

'Isn't Gary working today?' Claire asked, referring to the young man who worked at the store and helped with the heavy lifting.

'No, his wife, Sandy, just had a baby, remember?' Reginald said. 'Gary asked for a few days off so he could help her when she brings the baby home.'

'Oh, that's right,' Claire said, wishing

she could go with Reginald, but relieved that she wouldn't have Daniel dogging her footsteps all day.

'I'll probably walk over to the hospital and visit Dorothy sometime this morning,' Reginald continued. 'Perhaps the doctor will have some news about those tests.'

'I hope so,' Claire said. 'I need to stock up on groceries,' she told him. 'Dani and I can drive into town later and we'll stop in and visit Mom, then,' she said. 'By the way, what time on Friday does the viewing begin at the Braeside estate?'

'Doors open at ten, I believe,' Reginald replied. 'I've been thinking about that myself,' he said. 'If Dorothy's released from the hospital on Friday, I won't be able to go to the preview. You won't mind taking Daniel with you, will you?' he asked.

'Take me where?' Daniel asked, suddenly appearing behind them.

Claire felt her pulse pick up speed at the sound of his deep sensual voice. She curled her fingers around the mug in her hand and kept her eyes on Reginald.

'To view the house and contents of the Braeside estate,' Reginald explained.

'I'm looking forward to that,' Daniel said. 'But if transportation's a problem, I could always rent a car and find my own way there,' he offered.

'Nonsense,' Reginald declared. 'If Dorothy is released from the hospital, then you can go with Claire to the estate sale.'

Daniel nodded. 'I'll happily comply with whatever your plans are,' he said.

'I really appreciate you coming in with me this morning,' Reginald said. 'There's something I'd like to discuss with you.'

'No problem,' Daniel acknowledged, just as the telephone rang.

'I'll get it,' Reginald said.

'Would you like coffee or juice?' Claire politely asked Daniel as Reginald reached for the phone.

'Coffee, please' came the reply. 'But I

can help myself,' he added coolly.

Claire lifted her eyes to meet his, but his expression was unreadable. 'There's cereal or English muffins and fruit this morning,' she said, as she retrieved a coffee mug from the cupboard and set it on the counter in front of him. 'What can I get for you?'

'Thanks,' Daniel said as he removed the carafe from the coffee machine and began to fill the mug. 'I really don't expect you to wait on me,' he told her.

That there was a definite chill in Daniel's demeanor this morning was obvious, but after their set-to the previous evening she supposed she couldn't really blame him. For her part she'd spent the first half of the night telling herself she'd done the right thing and the second half wondering if she didn't at least owe him a chance to explain.

'I wasn't planning on playing waitress,' Claire replied, trying with difficulty to keep her tone even. 'Breakfast is a simple enough meal around here, and everyone usually helps themselves to whatever's on the table,' she told him. 'If you'll excuse me, I'll go and see if Dani's awake yet.' She turned and made her way from the kitchen.

Reginald replaced the phone receiver as she approached. 'The truck's arrived already,' he told her. 'That was the driver. He called from the coffee shop next door,' he explained.

'Are you sure you don't want me to come along?' Claire asked, wondering if Reginald might need more help. 'I can bring Dani. She doesn't mind playing in the store.'

'No, that's all right,' Reginald assured her. 'Daniel and I should manage just fine,' he said. 'We'd better grab a bite to eat and get going. See you later,' he added as Claire continued on her way.

* * *

For the next three days a pattern emerged. Each morning Daniel would accompany Reg to the store, to return home at approximately four in the afternoon. Claire and Dani spent the mornings completing various household chores and the afternoons driving into town to visit Dorothy and afterward browsing through the small local shopping mall picking out school supplies, or paying a visit to the library, one of Dani's favorite haunts.

Each evening after dinner Reginald paid his nightly visit to the hospital to see his wife. That he was still concerned about her welfare was apparent, but Claire had the distinct impression Reginald was wrestling with another problem, one he wasn't ready to talk to her about.

Daniel and Dani spent the evenings playing cards or croquet, or going for a walk along the stream that ran past the edge of the property. Though Claire was always invited to participate in these activities, she declined, using the excuse that she had paperwork to do for Reginald.

Daniel accepted her excuses without

comment and made no attempt to seek her out in order to put pressure on her to tell Dani the truth. While at times it seemed to Claire that he had given up on the issue, somehow his silence and deliberate avoidance of the subject served only to keep it constantly at the forefront of her mind.

Added to that was the fact that the relationship between Dani and her father was growing deeper and stronger with each passing day. There had been times during the past few days when Claire could easily have told Dani the truth about Daniel, but she hadn't been able to voice the words she knew would change their lives forever.

Daily she fought a war with her conscience, telling herself that by keeping Dani in the dark she was simply protecting the child. After all, what guarantee did she have that once the estate sale was over and Daniel returned to Boston to the commitments and responsibilities his business demanded, he would keep in contact with his daughter?

Resolutely refusing to acknowledge that she was only fooling herself, Claire continued to procrastinate, continued to avoid telling Dani the truth, fearful to face the real reason behind her reluctance, ignoring the voice inside her head telling her that when Daniel left she would miss him almost as much as Dani would.

It was on Thursday evening, while Dani and her father played croquet on the lawn outside, that Reginald joined Claire upstairs in the room they used as an office.

Glancing up from the list of new inventory she was feeding into the computer, Claire smiled a greeting.

'You must be looking forward to bringing Mom home tomorrow,' she said, guessing that this was the reason Reginald had been restless since his arrival home earlier that afternoon.

They had both been relieved to learn that the tests conducted on her mother earlier in the week had confirmed that no permanent damage had been done to her heart. As a result Dr. McGregor had given Dorothy the all clear and she was being released from the hospital in the morning.

'Yes, I am,' Reginald confirmed, but Claire could tell by the frown on her stepfather's face that he had something else on his mind.

'Is there something you want to talk to me about?' she asked, thinking that perhaps Reginald was ready to discuss what had been troubling him for the past few days.

'Yes, there is,' Reginald said as he came around the desk to stand at the window. He sighed heavily, avoiding her questioning gaze. 'Claire, first I want to say that I hope you won't think too ill of me. I realize I should have discussed this with you before now, especially after what your mother told me about you and ... ah ... your connection with Daniel — ' He broke off, his cheeks turning pink with embarrassment. 'But suffice it to say,' he hurried on with determination, 'I have been contemplating this step for quite some time. Your mother's heart attack simply brought the issue to a head.'

'What is it you're trying to tell me, Reg?' Claire asked, disturbed by the anxiety she sensed in him, and wondering at the shiver of apprehension that shimmied up her spine.

'This afternoon, Daniel made me an offer to take over the lease on the antique store as well as buy up all our current inventory,' Reg announced.

'What?' she said, unable to believe what she'd just heard. Shock and dismay flashed through her, making her head spin.

'I know ... this must come as something of a surprise,' Reginald said.

'Yes, it does,' Claire responded dazedly, praying that this was all a bad dream. She spun her chair around and rose to her feet. 'Reg? I mean are you sure this is what you want? Daniel hasn't been pressuring you — '

'Good heavens, no,' Reg quickly cut

in. 'I'm the one who approached him.' He paused and ran a hand across his face, obviously struggling for the words to explain. 'I've been thinking a lot about retirement lately, Claire,' he said evenly. 'Dorothy's heart attack . . . well . . . you could say it gave me the push I needed.' He turned to her, his blue eyes pleading for understanding. 'The thought that I might have lost her scared the heck out of me. I'm sixty-eight. It's high time I retired,' he stated. 'I want to spend every minute of the time we have left together with Dorothy. I love your mother more than I can say,' he continued, emotion thickening his voice and bringing tears to his eyes.

'I want to take her on a cruise around the world,' he went on. 'Just the two of us. No stress, no worries,' he explained. 'When I mentioned this in passing to Dr. McGregor he gave it the thumbs-up, said it was exactly what he'd prescribe. Your mother and I never had a proper honeymoon.' He ground to a halt and took a deep breath. 'I know this must seem like it's out of the blue, but I assure you, Claire, I've given this a great deal of thought. Please tell me that you understand.'

Claire was silent for a long moment, still trying to digest this astonishing news. She could see the worry etched on his features and knew he was anxious for her to give both her approval and support. But what she couldn't quite come to terms with was the fact that while she'd heard him talk about retirement before, she'd assumed he meant another five years down the road, perhaps longer. By then she'd hoped to have saved enough to buy into the business; then her plan had been to ask the bank for a loan, with the idea of eventually buying him out and becoming the store's owner herself.

'I . . . well . . . I am a little shocked,' she managed to say at last, trying unsuccessfully to hide the hurt she felt.

'Daniel was right,' Reginald said with a sigh. 'He wanted me to tell you from the start what we were discussing. But the timing never seemed to be right. And at first I wasn't sure Daniel would even consider making me an offer,' he went on. 'The fact that he'd been the one to fly us back to Peachville . . . well, I couldn't help thinking that fate had handed me a golden opportunity and I'd be a fool not to take advantage of the situation.' He paused, then hurried on. 'In case you're wondering, Daniel's assured me that your job won't be affected. He'll need you to manage the store for him.'

Reginald was gazing at her, his expression expectant. And suddenly Claire realized that her approval obviously meant a great deal to him. Throughout the past eight years he had been like a true father to her, giving her his love and his unconditional support. It was little enough to ask that she return the favor.

'If it's what you want, Reg, then I'm behind you one hundred percent,' Claire said, and watched as a look of both relief and joy lit up his features.

'Thank you, Claire,' Reg said. 'I knew I could count on you to understand and support me in this,' he said with a grateful smile. 'Now all I have to do is convince your mother to take that cruise. She doesn't know a thing about any of this,' he added. 'I didn't want to raise her hopes in case nothing came of it. I'm going to the hospital now to tell her the good news.'

'Give her my love,' Claire said, giving her stepfather a hug.

Once Reginald left, Claire crossed to the window and stood staring out at the sun as it made its slow descent behind the distant mountains. More than a little disconcerted by Reginald's disclosure, she struggled to keep the feelings of panic from surfacing, telling herself that her mother deserved the love and happiness Reginald seemed intent on giving her.

Her eyes were drawn to Daniel and Dani as they played their nightly game of croquet, and a wave of anger washed over her as her gaze came to rest on the man whose reappearance in her life continued to create havoc.

If what Reginald said was true, it was simply a matter of time before Daniel became the new owner of Farmer's Antiques, and her new boss. This thought sent a shiver of alarm racing through her.

Why had Daniel agreed to take over the lease? she wondered. Could it be that he had seen the opportunity as a means of bringing him closer to Dani?

Claire couldn't help thinking that under normal circumstances the likelihood of Reginald finding someone interested in taking over the antique store as speedily as he had would have been slim or none. But the alternative, to sell off the inventory to other dealers and terminate the lease of the store, would have taken considerably longer.

And while she couldn't fault Reginald for taking advantage of a situation, she resented the fact that the man he'd sold the business to was the last man on earth she'd have chosen to be her new boss.

Claire wiped away the stray tear tracing a path down her cheek and, turning from the window, returned to the computer terminal. Working for Daniel was quite simply out of the question. Impossible. She couldn't. She wouldn't. There was only one thing she could do, one action she could take. Clearing the screen, she began to type a letter of resignation.

With the experience she had and the contacts she'd made during the past few years, she felt confident that she would find another job in another town, ignoring the cry from her heart that said this was her home, this was where she and Dani belonged.

Ten minutes later, a tap at the door brought her attention away from the computer screen.

Daniel, wearing khaki baggy pants and a T-shirt with the logo Alexander Winery imprinted on it, stood in the doorway. Claire felt her heart kick against her ribs at the sight of him and she gritted her teeth in annoyance that her body seemed to have a will of its own whenever he appeared.

'Dani's in the bathtub,' he told her. 'I saw Reginald leave a little while ago and I wondered if he'd had a chance to talk to you.'

'Indeed he did,' Claire said testily.

'You're angry,' Daniel said, seeing the fiery glint in the depths of her blue eyes.

'Damn right, I'm angry,' Claire replied.

'And you're blaming me,' Daniel declared with a shake of his head. 'Claire, Reginald approached me, not the other way around,' he said. 'I thought he was kidding at first, but when I realized he was serious I tried to talk him out of it. He was adamant. He wanted out, for your mother's sake. That's when I made him the offer,' Daniel explained. 'I suppose you could say I happened to be in the right place at the right time.'

He watched as a cynical smile curled the edges of her mouth. 'Is that what happened in Camiore, too?' she asked. 'Were you in the right place at the right time?'

Daniel fought to hang on to his temper. She was upset and he couldn't really blame her for lashing out at him. 'What happened between us in Camiore has nothing whatsoever to do with this,' he said, managing to keep his tone even.

'It has everything to do with this,' Claire retorted, her voice rising. 'Taking over Reginald's store here in Peachville is simply your way of buying a place in Dani's life. But I've got news for you. It won't work, because if you think I'll stay here and work for you you're mistaken. I quit.'

'Claire, that's ridiculous. You're over-reacting. Taking over Reginald's store is strictly a business move, nothing more,' Daniel said, seeing the pain, anger and bewilderment in her eyes. 'You can't quit. I need you to look after things here. Reginald told me you're the best assistant he's ever had, that he's been grooming you to take over for him. Jobs are hard enough to come by these days without throwing one away just because you're angry at me.'

'Damn you. I can and I will,' Claire said defiantly, ignoring the voice in her head telling her Daniel was right, that she was overreacting. But ever since she'd set eyes on him at the auction in Vancouver less than a week ago, her world had been steadily spinning out of control and she couldn't seem to do a thing to stop it.

Daniel tried again. 'If you take time to think this through, Claire, you'll change your mind,' he said quietly, wishing now he'd waited until Dani was in bed before he'd sought her out.

'I'm not going to change my mind,' Claire shot back at him.

'You can be really stubborn at times. Do you know that?' He ran a hand through his hair in exasperation. 'You never give an inch, not even when you know you're in the wrong.'

'You're talking about something else now, aren't you? You're talking about my refusal to tell Dani?' she charged, her voice growing louder with every word.

'Claire, this isn't the time . . . ' Daniel replied, raising his hands in mock surrender.

'It's as good a time as any,' she told him, almost shouting at him now. 'So listen and listen good, because I'll only say it once. I'm not going to tell Dani that *you* are her father.'

Suddenly the sound of a strangled cry brought both their heads around. Dani, a towel wrapped haphazardly around her, her wet hair giving her a bedraggled puppy look, stared open-mouthed at the two of them.

Claire watched with growing horror as her daughter's beautiful gray eyes filled with tears.

Guilt and shame washed over her. 'Oh, Dani . . . darling!' Claire started to move toward her daughter.

'Is it true? Is Daniel my real daddy?' Dani asked as the tears spilled over to forge a path down her face.

Claire froze in midstride and her heart turned over at the confusion and pain she could see in her daughter's eyes. 'Yes, Daniel is your father,' Claire said softly, fighting back her own tears, hating herself for losing her temper and causing this disaster.

At her words, an array of emotions, ranging from astonishment, wonder and confusion flashed across Dani's face. 'Why didn't you tell me, Mommy?' Dani cried. 'Why didn't you tell me?' she wailed, her lower lip beginning to quiver.

'Dani . . . I . . . ' Claire began as she took another step toward her daughter.

'It's not fair. You lied to me. You should have told me the truth, Mommy! You should have told me!' Dani howled, her tears flowing faster now. Before Claire could respond, Dani turned and ran down the hall.

'No, Dani . . . wait!' Claire called out

as she headed to the door. She didn't get far. Daniel stepped in front of her, effectively blocking her path.

'Claire, I think Dani needs some time alone,' Daniel said, his hands restraining her.

'But I have to explain,' Claire said, fighting to hold back the tears stinging her eyes.

'She's not ready to hear your explanation yet,' Daniel said. 'She needs a little space, a little time to sort this out.'

Claire nodded, knowing he was right. Rushing after Dani now would only make matters worse.

'I'll go and check on her,' Daniel said. 'Will you be all right?' he asked. His tone was gentle, and for a heart-stopping moment Claire longed to feel his arms around her, longed to know the comfort of his embrace.

'I'll be fine,' she lied. Spinning away from him, she covered her mouth with her hand to stop the moan of pain and anguish bubbling to the surface.

Dear Lord, what have I done? What have I done? The question played over and over inside her head like a broken record. Why didn't I tell Dani coolly and calmly when I had the chance? Feelings of guilt overwhelmed her once more and she sank down into the chair, her face in her hands.

Why had she persisted in being such a stubborn fool? If only she'd told Dani at the start, this never would have happened, she berated herself dejectedly. If only. If only. Futile as it was, her wish brought neither comfort nor respite from the guilt churning inside her. And it was a bitter pill to swallow having to acknowledge that Daniel had been right.

But from the moment Dani was born and the nurse placed her baby in her arms, Claire had vowed to love and protect her daughter and provide a happy and secure home for her. She had done her best. But there had been times when being both mother and father had been challenging.

Daniel's reappearance in her life, and his genuine interest in his daughter, had caught her totally off guard, and as she'd watched the relationship between Dani and her father grow, a new and unwelcome emotion had enveloped her: fear. Fear of losing the one person who meant the world to her. Claire was afraid that by telling Dani that Daniel was her father, he would somehow supplant her in Dani's affections, and Dani would cease to love her mother.

Her refusal to tell Dani the truth had been motivated solely by that fear. And her mishandling of the situation had brought about exactly what she'd been desperate to avoid. The look in Dani's eyes had said it all. And now she wasn't sure if Dani would ever be able to forgive her.

Claire let the tears flow, vowing that she'd never again do anything to hurt her daughter. But would she get a second chance?

Daniel came to a halt in the doorway noting Claire's bent head and the

278

sadness emanating from her. A short time ago when Dani had discovered the truth, he'd been torn between the two, unsure just who needed him more, Claire or his daughter.

He'd followed his instincts, believing that Dani, hurt and angry because of Claire's deception, would need someone to comfort her, and who better than her own father. Dani had still been crying when he caught up with her in her bedroom. When he'd sat down on the bed beside her, she'd turned her tearstained face to look at him and with a muffled cry had thrown herself into his arms. His heart had spilled over with love for her, and he'd simply held her until the storm slowly abated.

He'd murmured words of comfort, telling Dani that her mother had been trying to protect her, and that sometimes out of love, adults made mistakes. Dani hadn't responded, and after tucking her into bed, he'd stroked her hair until her breathing deepened and she'd fallen asleep.

'Dani's asleep,' Daniel said as he quietly came up behind her.

Startled, Claire jumped at the sound of his voice and hurriedly wiped the wetness from her face. Outside, the night sky had turned a brilliant shade of pink, offering the promise of another sunny day.

'Go on, say it,' Claire said, keeping her back to him.

'Claire, don't,' Daniel said softly, hearing the pain and self-reproach in her voice.

'But you were right,' she said dejectedly, her shoulders slumping.

'All that matters is that Dani knows the truth,' he said, suddenly aching to comfort her. 'We just have to build on that,' he added as he watched her brush at another stray tear.

'Don't cry,' Daniel said, as he turned her to face him. 'You did what you thought was right. Don't beat yourself up about it,' he told her, but his words seemed to have little effect.

Placing his hand under her chin he

gently forced her to look at him. But the moment he saw the tears brimming in her eyes, his heart lurched painfully and, slipping his arms around her, he pulled her unresisting body against his.

All at once a wave of sensation washed over him as his senses were bombarded with the serenely seductive scent that was hers alone. He felt his stomach muscles tighten as an ache, slow and warm and sweetly sensual, began to spread through him. He'd forgotten how tiny and fragile she felt in his arms, forgotten, too, how dangerously alluring the feel of her body against his could be, igniting needs he found difficult to ignore.

Drawing a shaky breath he buried his face in the silky softness of her hair, reveling in the sudden and urgent desire pulsing through him. His heart was beating a rapid tattoo against his chest, and for a fleeting moment he wished he were back on a beach in Italy. With a moan of frustration, he held her at arm's length and gazed into eyes the color of moonbeams.

Claire felt her heart skid to a halt as Daniel looked deeply into her eyes. Then slowly, tantalizingly, he brought his mouth closer and closer until his lips claimed hers at last. Her sigh of pleasure was already lost in the wonder of his kiss, and as his tongue teased and tormented her, she moaned an urgent demand for more. Her heart was galloping like a mad thing, sending the blood coursing through her veins, awakening needs she'd all but forgotten.

She hadn't realized just how much she had hungered for the heat, how she'd craved to feel the power and how she'd yearned to experience just once more the dizzying desire suddenly rocketing through her. She'd forgotten the intoxicating taste of desire, one only he could ignite within her. And she'd forgotten, too, the incredible sweetness of his kiss, a kiss that drove her swiftly, too swiftly to the edge of reason. A kiss that touched her very soul.

The sensations vibrating through her only confirmed what she'd been denying for days. That she loved Daniel Hunter, had never stopped loving him. Because Daniel was her soul mate, the only man she would ever love.

This stunning realization acted like a splash of icy-cold water and she broke free of the kiss, twisting away from Daniel, fighting back a sob of despair.

'Claire, I'm sorry . . . ' At his words of apology Claire felt her heart shatter into a thousand pieces. Overcome with emotion she shook her head and hurried from the room.

Daniel didn't move. He stood in the darkening room for several long minutes waiting for his heart rate to return to normal, waiting for the need vibrating through him to slowly subside. Even after eight years she still had the power to tie him up in knots and send his system into overdrive.

When he'd pulled her into his arms he'd only meant to comfort her, but the moment he'd touched her he'd been lost as he'd suddenly found himself propelled back in time to that night eight years ago when he'd carried her out of the water and onto the beach.

He'd meant to comfort her then, too, knowing she'd been afraid for her life when she'd been pulled too far out to sea. But he'd been unable to resist the temptation of tasting her sweetness, touching her innocence and taking the gift she so generously gave, heedless of the consequences.

Daniel cursed furiously under his breath as the memory of those days in Camiore returned. He'd never met anyone quite like Claire, either before or since. Her youthful exuberance, her sharp wit, her sexy laugh and her incredible sense of wonder at the world around her, had captured his heart and restored his belief that dreams could come true.

She'd appeared like a nymph to lift his spirits and brighten his life at a time when he'd felt as if he'd lost his way. The reason he'd taken the side trip to

Camiore was to take stock of his life, reevaluate just where he was going and take the necessary steps to change the course he was on, a course mapped out for him by his father.

He'd been twenty-six that summer and not for the first time since becoming his father's right-hand man at Hunter Antiques, he'd began to resent the older man's sometimes domineering hand. He was well aware that he was being groomed to eventually step into his father's shoes and take over the reins of the business, but much as he loved his father, Daniel wasn't altogether sure he really wanted the job.

As far as his father was concerned, however, there were no ifs, ands or buts about it. But Daniel knew a confrontation was inevitable.

It wasn't that he didn't like the business or enjoy working with antiques. He did. But from an entirely different perspective. Instead of simply acquiring items for clients and selling them for a hefty profit, Daniel longed to seek out lost treasures with the intention of restoring them to their original beauty.

He'd seen his father pass up these abused treasures countless times, treasures that were often mistaken for garbage pieces, when he could see all that was needed was a little tender loving care, a little elbow grease, a little faith.

His grandfather had been the one who'd shown Daniel how to perform such transformations, and in doing so had instilled in him the joy of working with his hands. Each summer under his grandfather's watchful eye, Daniel would help him and practice his newfound skills working on an old dining room chair, or a beat-up piano stool, before allowing him to tackle larger and more challenging pieces.

Daniel loved the feeling of pride and accomplishment he'd experienced when the piece he'd worked on so painstakingly was restored almost to its original beauty. And it had been during those incredible days with

Claire, as he'd listened to her tell him her hopes and dreams for her future, that he'd finally realized that it was time for him to take the step he'd been contemplating for some time, to take charge of his own life and confront his father.

That had been his plan . . . but the accident to his father had effectively put an end to that dream and several others.

Marriage to Kelly had been another one of his father's ideas. William Hunter had wanted Daniel to marry the daughter of his best friend, and when Kelly's father died in the accident that critically injured Daniel's father, he'd suddenly found himself thrust into the role of comforting not only his mother and brother, but Kelly, as well.

Kelly's mother had died shortly after Kelly was born and her father had doted on his daughter ever since, giving her everything her heart desired. Daniel and Kelly had been friends, and had dated a number of times, but the death of her adored father had affected her profoundly. She'd turned to Daniel for the comfort and guidance her father had always provided and had become overly dependent on him.

The fact that Claire hadn't bothered to get in touch with him and the constant worry of his father's slow recuperation had left Daniel feeling emotionally vulnerable, and he'd simply drifted into a relationship with Kelly, a relationship that had the added pressure of her dependency on him.

She'd told him she was in love with him, and he supposed that she truly believed that to be true, and while he had cared for her very much he hadn't been entirely sure that what he felt was love.

Though Daniel's father's recovery had been slow, William had continually pointed out that Kelly would make Daniel a good wife, a loving life companion, and that it was time for him to settle down and start a family of his own.

He'd bought into the fantasy and proposed to Kelly, who'd immediately accepted. And suddenly he'd found himself on a fast-moving train as plans and preparations were set in motion.

It was ironic, he thought with a shake of his head, that on the morning of his wedding day he'd woken up from a dream in which Claire had walked out of the ocean and into his arms.

What would have happened, he wondered with a beleaguered sigh, if he'd been the one to answer the door that day to find her standing outside, a baby in her arms?

10

Claire lay in her bed, staring up at the ceiling, her thoughts in chaos, her heart in turmoil. Disasters tended to strike unexpectedly, and the one she'd just been a witness to was no exception.

Everything had happened so fast. From Reginald's announcement about the takeover of the business and her subsequent argument with Daniel, to the sudden appearance of Dani at a most inopportune moment. And last, but certainly not least, the kiss.

A shiver ran through her as the memory of those moments when she'd been held by Daniel and kissed by Daniel flashed into her mind. The overwhelming feeling that this was where she belonged, that she'd finally come home, had caught her totally off guard.

And when his lips touched hers she'd

been instantly transported to that plane of existence that only lovers know, where only lovers go . . . and eight years had simply fallen away, taking her back to a beach in Italy where the man of her dreams had walked out of the water and into her heart.

She'd never believed in love at first sight, until that moment. But that's what had happened, and in the days that followed she'd thought Daniel felt exactly the same. She'd been wrong. Daniel had had a girlfriend tucked away back home, a girlfriend he'd omitted to tell Claire about, a girlfriend he'd ultimately married.

The warmth and tenderness he'd shown her had been a lie. Their brief relationship had been built on a lie, and the confidence and courage he'd helped instill in her had been stripped away when he failed to appear in Paris as he'd promised.

Timing, setting and circumstance and her own longing for true love had undoubtedly clouded her thinking.

She'd been caught up in emotions so strong, she'd naively assumed they were returned in kind. But Daniel had never spoken the words she'd yearned to hear, the words that would have bound her to him forever.

And for the past eight years she'd repeatedly reminded herself that what had happened between them had been nothing more than a holiday romance. What she'd felt for Daniel had simply been a case of infatuation brought on by the attention of a handsome and experienced man.

The passage of time had helped her bury the feelings she'd once reveled in, and she'd even managed to convince herself that what she'd felt for Daniel hadn't been love at all.

But she'd been wrong. Horribly wrong. From the moment she'd set eyes on him again, her heart had responded with a welcoming leap and her emotions had awakened as if from a long sleep.

His touching concern for her mother's welfare, his act of kindness in flying her and Reginald home and his determination to get to know his daughter, had chipped away at the wall she'd built around her heart.

But the quiet patience and gentle understanding he'd shown his daughter, and the obvious joy Dani's very existence brought him, had effectively worn down the remnants of resistance that remained.

And the emotion that had burst free of the confines she'd forcibly put on it so long ago, the emotion still thrumming through her veins, could no longer be ignored or contained.

Claire closed her eyes against the pain clutching at her insides. She loved Daniel, had never stopped loving him and her love was as strong, if not stronger, than it had been eight years ago when he'd walked into her life.

But even as she finally accepted this realization, she quickly reminded herself that Daniel's presence in Peachville was solely due to Dani, the child, until only a few days ago, he hadn't known he'd fathered.

The tragic loss of his infant son had unquestionably heightened his need to form a relationship with Dani, but Claire knew in her heart that Daniel's commitment to his daughter was deep and lasting.

But what about her? Where did she fit into the picture? Claire's mouth twisted into a sad smile. The tumultuous kiss they'd shared had evolved out of an emotionally charged moment, nothing more. Daniel had simply been offering comfort, that was all, and if she was foolish enough to entertain the notion that he had designs on rekindling their relationship, his apology following the kiss had firmly squashed that faint hope.

* * *

Claire, wearing an apron over her green silk blouse and loose navy skirt, had been working in the kitchen for more than an hour when Reginald joined her.

'Something smells good,' he said as he poured himself a cup of coffee.

'I made some banana muffins for breakfast and an apple pie for Mom's homecoming dinner,' Claire explained as she donned oven gloves and removed the sumptuous-looking pie from the oven.

'Mmm. She'll like that,' Reginald said. 'I know she's really looking forward to coming home today,' he added.

'And we're looking forward to having her home, too,' Claire said as she set the pie on the cooling tray, the smell of cinnamon permeating the room.

'Last night I talked to your mother about Daniel taking over the business,' Reginald said as Claire turned off the oven and picked up the glass of orange juice from the counter nearby.

'What did she say?' she asked.

'She didn't believe me at first,' her stepfather replied. 'But after a while I managed to convince her that I wasn't pulling her leg,' he went on. 'And guess what?'

'What?' Claire obliged, taking another sip of the sweet juice.

'She says she's always wanted to go on a cruise,' he said with a laugh. 'Can you believe that?'

'That's great,' Claire replied, managing a smile.

'She was a bit concerned about you, until I told her Daniel had promised me you'd still have a job, that he'd need you to take over as manager,' Reginald went on. 'That reassured her somewhat.'

Claire was silent. She'd done a good deal of thinking since last night, acknowledging that she had overreacted when she'd told Daniel she wanted to quit. In retrospect she'd decided to stay on. The main factor in her decision had been that Daniel would have to return to Boston at some point in the near future, and once he was gone, she could only hope that their lives would return to some semblance of order.

'Mmm . . . something smells good.' The sound of a deep masculine voice brought Claire out of her reverie, and she turned to see Daniel, with Dani at his side, come into the kitchen.

Claire felt her heart give an all-too-familiar leap at the sight of him, wearing beige cotton slacks and a multicolored short-sleeved shirt, his black hair combed back off his forehead, accentuating the strong planes and angles of his handsome face.

'Morning,' Reginald said jovially. 'Claire's been baking,' he added. 'She's almost as good a cook as her mother, you know,' he teased as he helped himself to a muffin from the basket on the counter.

Heart pounding, Claire watched Dani climb onto her chair. She smiled tentatively at her daughter, but Dani's face curled into a frown and she dropped her gaze, deliberately avoiding looking at Claire, turning instead to say something to Daniel, who'd sat down on the chair beside her.

A pain sharp and intense stabbed at Claire's heart. Even though she knew Dani had every right to be angry, that Claire deserved the cold-shoulder treatment being meted out, didn't make Dani's snub any easier to take.

'I made your favorite muffins, Dani,' Claire said as she set the basket of warm muffins on the table.

'I'm not hungry,' Dani declared, keeping her eyes averted.

'Well, I am,' Daniel said, flashing Claire a sympathetic smile as he reached for a muffin.

'I suppose you're taking Dani to the viewing with you,' Reginald said, as he pulled out the chair at the head of the table and sat down.

'Yes,' Claire replied. She'd tried for the past few days to find a sitter, but she'd had no luck.

'I've only been inside the Braeside estate once,' Reginald said. 'But if my memory serves me well, there are some great quality pieces, most of them John Foreman brought with him from

Scotland back in the early 1920s,' he went on. 'That's why there's bound to be a good turnout today.'

'Do I have to go?' Dani asked, addressing the question to her father and not Claire.

'You just might enjoy yourself,' he told her easily, flashing a smile. 'And when your mother and I are finished looking over everything, maybe we'll have time to stop off at Rainbow Lake on the way home and go for a quick swim,' he added.

Dani's expression swiftly changed and she smiled at her father. Claire felt her heart twist painfully at the brief exchange. Reginald, busily buttering his muffin, seemed unaware of the tension between Claire and Dani as he reached for the pot of jam.

'By the way,' Reginald said, glancing at Daniel, 'I've been meaning to tell you that Alan Blakely called yesterday and he asked me to pass along an invitation to drop by anytime. He wants to thank you in person for giving him the chance to buy that player piano.'

Claire threw Daniel a startled glance. She'd forgotten about her botched attempt to buy the player piano for Alan, and she was surprised and pleased that Daniel had offered to let Alan buy back the piece for his collection.

'I'd like that,' Daniel said.

'Alan's got quite a collection,' Reginald said. 'And he loves to show people around. Maybe you can fit in a visit before you head back to Boston.'

At his remark Claire saw Dani's eyes widen in surprise and confusion. Claire could easily read the thoughts flashing across her daughter's face. Had she just found her father only to have him leave?

'Well, I think I'll head into town and run a few errands before I pick Dorothy up at the hospital.' Reginald dabbed at his mouth with his napkin. 'I'll look forward to hearing all about the viewing when you get back,' he added.

After Reginald had gone, Dani, who hadn't eaten anything, but simply sipped at her glass of juice, hopped down from her chair. 'When are we leaving?' Her question was directed at Daniel and Claire bit back the reprimand that sprang to her lips.

Daniel glanced over at Claire, his dark eyebrows rising in silent query.

'Viewing starts at ten,' she told him. She glanced at the clock on the opposite wall. 'It's nine o'clock now. We should leave here in about twenty minutes,' she said.

Dani didn't bother to look around, her gaze remained focused on her father as she waited for him to answer. 'Be ready in twenty minutes,' he told her.

'Can you come and help me find my bathing suit in case we go to the lake, Da . . . Daniel?' Dani asked, her tone bordering on babyish now.

The slight but deliberate hesitation wasn't lost on Claire. Dani had been about to say Daddy, only changing it to Daniel at the last second.

'Sure,' said Daniel easily. 'But when

that's done I need to make a couple of telephone calls before we go,' he added as he, too, rose from his chair. 'How about we meet you at the car in twenty minutes?' he suggested to Claire as Dani led the way from the kitchen.

'Fine,' Claire replied, blinking away the tears stinging her eyes.

Claire busied herself clearing away the breakfast dishes before preparing the cabbage for the coleslaw that would accompany the barbecued salmon steaks she'd bought for Dorothy's homecoming meal.

That Dani seemed intent on continuing to give Claire the silent treatment was even more apparent a short time later when she ignored her mother and climbed into the back seat of the car, her small tote bag in her hand.

'All set?' Claire asked as she took her seat behind the wheel.

Dani scowled, making no response, and it was Daniel who answered 'I think so,' as he settled into the passenger seat beside her.

Claire fought back a sigh as she put the car into gear and headed down the driveway. No one spoke as she took the route that skirted the edge of town and brought them to a crossroads. There they made a left turn onto the road that would take them to Braeside estate.

Outside, the sun shone down from an azure blue sky and Claire was thankful of the car's air-conditioning. The silence hung over her like a dark cloud, and not for the first time she wished she could turn back the clock and change the decision she'd made not to tell Dani the truth. Dani's punishment was working well, Claire thought as she flipped the visor down to block out the bright sun before negotiating a curve.

Traffic was busy as the string of cars appeared to be heading in the same direction. Tired and more than a little frustrated, Claire broke the silence.

'Rumor has it that when John Foreman, the late owner of Braeside estate, brought his bride to Canada, she instantly fell in love with the new land,' she said. 'They built the house known as Braeside a year or two after they arrived in this part of British Columbia. Unfortunately, they never had any children,' she added.

'Really,' Daniel said, his tone showing his interest. 'What line of work was Mr. Foreman in?' he asked.

'He was an architect and builder just like his father,' said Claire. 'He was originally from the Edinburgh area, I believe,' she added. 'His father was said to have owned a successful contracting business, until a fire destroyed a group of homes they were building and they lost every penny. And that's when his father told John he had to marry into money, that it was his duty to do what he had to to help them rebuild their business. He'd even picked the girl out,' she explained.

'Who was she?' Daniel asked.

'The daughter of a rich landowner,' Claire told him. 'But John refused, because he was in love with a young farm girl he'd met at a country fair, and unbeknownst to his father, had already proposed to the girl and been accepted.'

'That must have caused an uproar,' Daniel commented dryly.

'And how,' said Claire warming up to the story now. She wasn't sure just how much of it was actually true. She'd heard the tale a number of times since moving to Peachville, and each time it was slightly different. 'When his father found out about Helen, he demanded that John forget her, saying he'd disown him if he didn't obey. That's when John and his beloved Helen eloped. Six months later they emigrated to Canada.'

'But how did he take all these antiques — all the furniture — with him?' Daniel asked.

'Ah . . . but there's the twist,' Claire said, smiling a little now. 'You see, the furniture actually belonged to his new bride,' she said. 'It turned out that Helen's father hadn't been as poor as everyone believed. He died a few months after the elopement, leaving everything to his daughter.'

Daniel laughed, the deep low rumble of sound sending a shiver of awareness chasing through Claire.

Putting on the car signal, she followed the line of vehicles making the turn into the long driveway leading to John and Helen Foreman's house.

'Reginald wasn't kidding when he said there'd be a good turnout for this,' Daniel said when Claire brought the car to a halt in one of the fields adjacent to the building.

They climbed out and began to make their way to the house.

'Mommy, Mommy,' Dani blurted out, before breaking off abruptly. 'I mean, Daniel. Look, there's Mark. You remember him? You met him at Rainbow Lake.'

Claire, encouraged and warmed by Dani's slip, said nothing, but followed the direction of her daughter's gaze to see Mark Alexander waving frantically at them from the rear window of a car. The car, driven by a beautiful dark-haired woman, slowed to a halt as it neared them.

'Hi, Claire. Hi, Dani.' The woman greeted them with a warm smile.

'Hello, Kit. How are you?' Claire asked.

'I'm fine,' came the reply. 'I just dropped Nathan off at the door a second ago,' she went on. 'He wanted to take a quick look around. It looks like the whole town's shown up,' she added as a group of people walked around the car and headed toward the house.

'We're going to take a look around, too,' Claire said. 'Kit, I'd like you to meet Daniel Hunter, of Hunter Antiques in Boston,' she went on. 'Daniel, this is Kit Alexander. She runs a photography studio in town. Her husband, Nathan, owns Alexander Winery. That's where those wines are made that Reginald is always raving about.'

'And quite rightly, too,' Daniel said. 'Mrs. Alexander, it's my pleasure,' he added, flashing one of his charismatic smiles.

'It's nice to meet you,' Kit said. 'And please, call me Kit. Oh, by the way, Claire, how's your mother? Is she home from hospital yet?'

'Reginald's gone to pick her up this morning,' Claire said. 'And she's doing just fine, thanks.'

'That's great,' Kit replied. 'Give her my love and tell her Joyce will be dropping by to see her soon. Yes, Mark, what is it?' She turned to the boy in the back seat who'd been tapping her shoulder.

'Can Dani come with us to the lake?' Mark asked.

Kit glanced up at Claire. 'I'm taking Mark to his swimming lessons,' she explained. 'You're certainly welcome to come and watch if you like Dani,' Kit said.

'Can I go? Please?' Dani asked, directing her question out of habit to Claire, her earlier animosity forgotten, at least for the moment.

'It's fine with me, but I hate to impose,' Claire said.

'Don't be silly,' Kit assured her. 'The only problem is I won't be coming back this way to pick Nathan up — he's getting a ride home later with Charlie Fisher. If you don't mind taking a side trip, you can pick Dani up at the house when you've finished here,' she suggested.

'That might be a few hours,' Claire said.

'No problem. Mark will enjoy the company. Come by whenever you're ready,' Kit said as a horn blared behind her. 'Quick, get in,' she told Dani, who had brought her tote bag with her from the car. Seconds later Kit waved as she drove off.

'She's nice,' Daniel said as they joined the lineup of people making their way inside the house.

'Yes, she is,' Claire replied. 'Listen, we're bound to get separated in there,' she went on. 'Why don't we each pick up a catalog and go around on our own and compare notes later?' she suggested.

'Sounds like a good idea,' Daniel said.

Once inside the house, Claire, after paying for the catalog at the door, quickly made her way upstairs to the bedrooms. She was glad Daniel didn't follow her. She preferred to work on her own and was interrupted only occasionally by someone stopping to say hello or to ask after her mother's health.

She made extensive notes as she roamed from room to room. Many of the pieces, such as the enormous mahogany wardrobe in the master bedroom and the two mirrored dressers, one from each of the other bedrooms, were in mint condition.

As she wandered through the large house, from kitchen to attic, she jotted down which pieces she thought might interest several of the store's regular customers.

She couldn't help feeling a certain sadness for John Foreman and his wife,

Helen. One of the small bedrooms on the top floor would have been ideal for a child, she thought, as she crossed to stand at the window looking out at a giant oak tree, its branches reaching out to the house to gently brush the windows.

But it was the master bedroom with its turret design and the gleaming hardwood floors that somehow captured her imagination and her heart. The bed itself was covered with one of the most beautiful handmade quilts she'd ever seen. The variety of patterned squares with intricately sewn designs took her breath away.

And it was here that Daniel found her several hours later, staring out across the grounds, a look of sadness on her face.

'I thought I might find you here,' said Daniel in a soft voice as he came to stand beside her at the window.

Claire felt her heart jam against her breastbone at his words. 'It's a beautiful room,' she managed to say, feeling the blood rush to her cheeks.

'And a fabulous house,' he commented. 'I'm starving. How about you?' he went on as several people joined them in the room.

'Mmm-hmm,' she said, suddenly realizing that she was indeed hungry.

'What do you say we compare notes over lunch, then pick up Dani when we're done?' he suggested.

'All right,' Claire said as she walked with him from the house and across the field to the car.

'Why don't you let me drive?' he offered. 'Just point me in the direction of the nearest restaurant,' he added.

'Okay,' Claire replied, warmed by his offer. Tossing Daniel the keys to the car, she settled into the passenger seat.

'To get to Meadowvale you have to head back to the crossroads and go straight through,' Claire said as she buckled her seat belt. 'Just follow the signs,' she instructed. 'There are a few nice places on the main street that serve a decent lunch.'

'Fine. I think I can find my way there,' he replied. 'Close your eyes and relax. You look like you could use a rest,' he said as he maneuvered the car down the driveway.

Claire nodded, surprised to discover that she did feel a trifle weary. The steady hum of the engine, together with the warm sun beating in through the windows, brought a sleepy sigh to her lips. Taking Daniel's advice, she closed her eyes.

It seemed only seconds later that Claire was aroused from her slumber by a feather-light kiss on her lips. She opened her eyes to see Daniel, his face scarcely an inch from hers, a look she couldn't fathom lurking in the gray eyes.

His smile sent her heart into a tailspin and her lungs seemed to have forgotten their purpose as her breath locked in her throat.

'I've always wanted to awaken a sleeping princess,' he said, and at the husky timbre of his voice Claire thought her bones had somehow melted, as a glorious weakness claimed her.

Claire glanced outside, realizing that they'd reached Meadowvale and were in fact parked on the main street. 'We're here. I . . . I must have fallen asleep,' she murmured, pushing away the lethargy that was making it difficult for her to move.

'You obviously needed it,' Daniel said, moving away. 'So, where shall we eat?'

'There's a nice bistro just down the street,' she said, finally managing to pull her scattered wits about her.

The bistro was busy but they soon found a table in the corner. After the waitress had taken their order of a deviled egg sandwich and Caesar salad for Claire, and a ham on rye and green salad for Daniel, they sipped contentedly from the glasses of ice-cold water the waitress had brought when she'd shown them to their table.

Claire brought out her catalog and

Daniel listened as she pointed out the pieces she thought were worth bidding for, explaining her reasons for each selection. Daniel agreed with her on almost all of the choices, including several unique kitchen items; a maple antique rolling pin, two Brown Betty pottery cream jugs, a silver-plated toast rack and a beautiful copper kettle.

Daniel, in turn, asked her opinion of several larger items, and much to her surprise most of the pieces he had chosen were on her own list. But knowing Reginald's tendency to shy away from these she hadn't mentioned them. She was also astonished to discover that some of the pieces he recommended not only needed to be repaired, but refinished.

'Unfortunately, there isn't anyone in this area who does refinishing,' Claire said a few minutes later, after the waitress set their respective lunches in front of them.

'I plan on doing the refinishing myself,' Daniel said before taking a bite of his sandwich.

'You?' Claire couldn't hide her surprise. 'Do you know how? I mean . . . where did you learn — ' she broke off, feeling her face grow hot with embarrassment. She'd assumed that like a large number of people in the antique business, he was simply a buyer and seller of the goods, avoiding items of poorer quality or ones in need of repair.

'My grandfather taught me,' Daniel said. 'That's how Hunter Antiques got started,' he went on. 'My grandfather had been taught by his father, and gradually over a period of time people began asking him to fix and restore items. My grandfather had a gift,' he said, pride and love echoing in his words. 'My father was the one who saw the potential of simply buying better-quality items and selling them for a higher price.'

'Your grandfather taught you?' Claire asked, enjoying listening to Daniel telling a little of his family history.

'Yes,' he replied, a smile tugging at the corners of his mouth. 'Every year my brother and I would spend our summer vacations with my grandparents in Ontario. I used to love to watch him working and he often let me help. It was incredibly exciting to watch a piece of furniture transformed to almost mint condition. I'll never forget it.'

'Before I started working for Reginald, he had an employee who did minor repairs,' Claire said. 'Sometimes he'd tackle a bigger job of stripping down a dresser or a table and restoring it,' she went on. 'Reg always said you needed a lot of patience to really do a good job.'

'He's right,' Daniel said. 'But unfortunately we're a throwaway society these days,' he added. 'If something doesn't look right, or people get tired of things that look old or battered, they just throw them away and buy something new. I think it's criminal.'

'I do, too,' Claire said.

'It's been a dream of mine for a long

time to get back to working with my hands the way my grandfather once did,' Daniel continued, his tone wistful, his expression thoughtful. 'It's a dream I intend to fulfill,' he added with quiet determination.

'Really,' Claire replied, thinking that she'd never heard Daniel speak so passionately about anything before. Eight years ago he hadn't been much of a talker, and even when they had talked, it had been about superficial subjects, nothing too deep or profound. Besides, she'd been too much in love, too high on the feelings he'd so easily aroused in her, to think straight.

'Rebuilding and restoring,' Daniel repeated. 'There's a lot to be said for it, don't you agree?'

Claire met his gaze and for a fleeting moment she wasn't altogether sure if he was still talking about antiques. There was a glint of something indefinable in the depths of his eyes, making her breath catch in her throat and her pulse pick up speed.

She watched as Daniel dropped his gaze and began to toy with the remains of his salad. 'Sitting here with you like this brings back memories of Italy,' he said softly, and Claire felt her heart skip a beat at his words.

'That was a long time ago,' she managed to say, as she curled her fingers around the water glass.

'You're right. It was,' he agreed with a rueful smile. 'But I really did plan to meet you in Paris,' he went on.

Claire was silent, waiting to feel the familiar surge of anger, but to her surprise it didn't materialize.

'I dropped the note off on my way to the airport,' he continued. 'The taxi driver didn't want to make the detour, he kept insisting there wasn't a Château L'est Hotel, but when I promised him an extra hundred francs, he soon found it,' said Daniel as he pushed his plate aside.

Claire felt her heart jolt against her rib cage. 'Château L'est? We weren't staying at the Château L'est Hotel,' she said in disbelief. 'We were at the Château L'ouest,' she told him.

Daniel was silent for a long moment, his expression unreadable. 'East is east and west is west and never the twain shall meet,' Daniel recited, his eyes on Claire, his expression thoughtful now. 'That would certainly explain things,' he added, his mouth twisting in an ironic smile.

Claire couldn't speak. She felt totally numb. The only explanation she could come up with for what must have happened, was that she'd either given Daniel the wrong name or perhaps he'd written it down wrong.

A simple mistake. An easy one to make, especially when the language was foreign, *est* being the French word for east and *ouest* the French word for west. But the consequences in this case had been far-reaching indeed.

'Do you want to know what I said in my note?' he asked, breaking into her musings.

As she lifted her gaze to meet his she

was suddenly swamped with feelings of guilt and regret. She'd refused to listen, refused to believe. She owed him the chance to explain. She nodded.

'My father had been badly hurt in a car accident back home,' he told her, his voice calm, his tone unaffected. 'There was a message to that effect waiting for me when I arrived at my hotel in Paris. I called my mother and got the news that my father was on the critical list. I immediately booked a flight home and then wrote a letter telling you why I had to leave.'

'Daniel, I'm so sorry,' Claire said, as her feelings of guilt compounded at his words.

'Tom Albright, a business associate of my father's, died at the scene,' Daniel continued. 'My father remained on the critical list for several days. My mother was frantic with fear and worry and then thankfully they told us he was out of danger and on the road to recovery.'

Albright. The name was familiar. And suddenly Claire remembered that Kelly

Albright had been named in the marriage announcement she'd read on the plane back from Boston. Kelly Albright was the woman Daniel had married that day in June when Claire had brought Dani to meet her father.

All at once the joy she'd felt only a few moments ago evaporated like steam from a kettle. Nothing had really changed.

'It must have been awful for you,' Claire managed to say, all the while fighting to maintain her composure, silently telling herself that they couldn't go back, that even if she'd known about the reason he'd left Paris, the fact still remained that a woman named Kelly Albright had had a previous claim on Daniel, a claim he hadn't bothered to mention.

'It was a difficult time for everyone, especially Kelly,' Daniel said, effectively reinforcing Claire's belief.

'Life goes on,' Claire said, beginning to wish they'd never started the trip down memory lane. But while part of her was glad to learn that he had tried to contact her, that he had written a note explaining his disappearance, another part of her wished she hadn't discovered the unfortunate mistake.

'Claire, listen.' Daniel's tone was urgent and he reached across the table to take her hand in his. 'I know we can't go back. We can't change what happened,' he said as his fingers gently massaged hers. 'What's important now is Dani, her happiness, her well-being, right?'

'Yes, but — '

'Then I have the perfect solution,' he quickly cut in. 'Let's get married.'

11

Claire stared in stunned disbelief at Daniel. 'What did you say?' she asked, her tone breathless, her heart kicking crazily against her breastbone.

'I said, let's get married,' Daniel repeated, and at his words the water glass in Claire's hand slid through her trembling fingers to catch the edge of her plate and spill its contents over the table and onto her lap.

'Oh . . . no . . . ' Pushing back her chair, Claire leapt to her feet.

The waitress hurried to their table. 'Are you all right?' she asked, as she began mopping up the water.

'I'm fine,' Claire replied, feeling her face grow hot with embarrassment, aware that everyone in the restaurant had turned to stare at her. 'Excuse me,' she murmured before heading off in the direction of the washroom.

Once inside the small room Claire slid the bolt closed and leaned heavily against the door, taking several deep steadying breaths. After a few moments she lifted her gaze to focus on her reflection in the mirror above the sink, seeing the look of hope, the look of longing, flickering in the depths of her blue eyes.

She hadn't been dreaming. Daniel had actually suggested they get married. But even as a surge of joy exploded through her, Claire quickly brought the emotion to a heel, reminding herself, that Daniel had simply presented the idea as a solution, *the perfect solution* was what he'd said. There had been no mention of love, no reference to emotions, no declaration of feelings, no promise of happiness.

Claire bit down on the inner softness of her mouth to stop the sob threatening to burst free. She dropped her gaze and, plucking several paper towels from the dispenser on the wall, began dabbing at the wetness on her skirt, silently berating herself for being a prize fool.

For a heart-stopping moment she'd allowed herself to dream. She'd bought into the romantic fantasy of living happily ever after. But it wasn't to be. Daniel simply regarded marriage as a solution, a solution that would give him total and unlimited access to his daughter. A marriage of convenience. A marriage without love.

Claire tossed the paper towel into the garbage and ran her hands under the cool water before gently patting her face. She glanced at her reflection once more and this time was relieved to note that her expression revealed none of the pain or emotional turmoil going on inside her.

Drying her hands and face, she unlocked the door and made her way back to the table. Daniel rose as she approached and she glimpsed a look of concern in his eyes — concern and something more, something she couldn't easily interpret.

'I've taken care of the check,' he told her before she could sit down. 'I thought perhaps we should pick up Dani,' he added.

Claire managed a brief smile. 'Fine,' she replied and continued on toward the door and out into the street.

'I'll drive,' she told him, wanting to have something with which to occupy her mind, something to keep her thoughts at bay.

Daniel handed her the keys as they reached the car, and as their fingers briefly made contact, it was all Claire could do not to jerk her hand away.

With a nonchalance she was far from feeling, she slid behind the wheel and fastened her seat belt. After starting the engine she put the car into reverse and backed out of the parking space, before continuing along the main street.

'Claire, I know marriage is a serious undertaking,' Daniel said, breaking into the tense silence. 'But I really think we could make it work,' he added as Claire slowed the car at the junction leading out of Meadowvale.

Claire's throat was bone dry. She couldn't answer. Loving him as she did, she was torn between wanting desperately to say yes to his unorthodox proposal, yet all the while knowing that he was only asking her as a means to an end, and not because he truly loved and wanted her.

'Is there someone else?' Daniel spoke again, frustrated by her silence and more than a little panicked that she seemed so cool and controlled, revealing no emotion whatsoever, at least none that he could see. 'I mean . . . I know that you've been seeing that real-estate fellow, Rick . . . but I got the impression the relationship was relatively new, that you weren't exactly contemplating marriage. Was I wrong?'

Claire was tempted for a moment to lie, to tell him that she was very interested in Rick, that they had spoken about marriage, but she couldn't force the words past the dryness in her throat.

Daniel cursed under his breath, surprised at just how much he wanted her to agree to his suggestion, surprised, too, at the stab of jealousy he felt at the thought that he might have been wrong, that there was more to her relationship with Rick Robson.

Maybe he was being a bit selfish, he acknowledged. But marriage seemed the perfect solution. After all, they were Dani's biological parents and they both cared deeply about the child. He felt confident Dani would adjust quickly to the situation, sure that his daughter had come to care for him as much as he cared for her.

'Will you at least think about what I've said?' Daniel asked, more than a hint of exasperation in his voice. 'I don't want to pressure you, but I'd really like to have an answer before I head back to Boston,' he said.

Claire maintained her silence as she took the turnoff leading to Alexander Winery. She needed to think, needed to explore both the pros and cons of such an alliance before making a decision that would affect their lives forever.

'All right,' she said at last as she brought the car to a halt at the end of the driveway. 'I'll think about it and let you know.'

Kit Alexander answered their knock, greeting them with a welcoming smile.

'Come on in,' she invited. 'The children took the dogs for a walk. They'll be back shortly,' she told them as they followed her into the spacious kitchen.

'Nathan, darling. Claire and Daniel are here,' Kit announced as they joined him in the kitchen.

'Claire, it's nice to see you. How are you?' Nathan asked, his smile friendly.

'Fine, thanks,' she replied. 'Nathan, I'd like you to meet Daniel Hunter. He's an antique dealer from Boston,' she added, opting to keep the introduction simple.

'From Hunter Antiques, by any chance?' Nathan asked as he extended his hand to Daniel.

'Yes,' Daniel confirmed. As he and Nathan shook hands, each man eyed the other with obvious interest. 'We met your wife after she'd dropped you off at the viewing today,' Daniel continued. 'I gather you're also interested in antiques.'

Nathan nodded. 'On a somewhat smaller scale,' he explained. 'I collect antique corkscrews and other wine-related paraphernalia,' he said.

'Really,' Daniel replied.

'Darling, perhaps Daniel would enjoy a tour of the winery, and a peek at your corkscrew collection,' Kit suggested. 'Claire and I will have a visit on the patio and watch for the children,' she added.

'I'd be happy to give a guided tour,' Nathan said. 'But only if you're interested, of course.'

'I'd love it. Thank you,' Daniel said. 'Wines are another passion of mine and during the past week I've tasted several from your winery,' he went on. 'I must say that I'm very impressed. They're truly exceptional.'

'Thank you,' Nathan replied, flashing a smile of appreciation. 'Reginald is a long-standing customer and he's as good a judge of wines as he is of antiques,' he commented as he led Daniel from the kitchen.

'Would you like a glass of homemade lemonade?' Kit asked Claire once the men had departed.

'Mmm . . . that sounds wonderful,' Claire replied.

'I made some for Dani and Mark when we got back from Rainbow Lake,' Kit said as she brought the pitcher from the fridge and filled two tall glasses. 'Let's sit outside,' she went on, crossing to open the door leading to the red-tiled patio.

'How was the swimming lesson?' Claire asked, sitting down on one of the four lawn chairs that surrounded a rectangular table with a brightly colored umbrella.

'Great. Mark loves the water and he's doing well,' Kit replied. 'But what he really wants to do is learn how to dive,' she went on. 'He was telling me about Daniel teaching Dani how to dive.'

'Yes, he did,' Claire said before taking a sip of the refreshing drink.

'Claire . . . ' Kit said tentatively. 'I hope you won't think I'm being nosy.' She stopped.

Claire turned to look at her friend.

'It's just that I heard Dani and Mark talking in the back seat on the way home from the lake,' Kit continued. 'Dani said something about her father being here, that he'd come to pay her a visit . . . '

Claire felt the blood drain from her face and she set the glass of lemonade on the table in front of her. Of course Dani was bound to talk about Daniel. Hadn't the subject of her father fascinated her from the time she'd learned to talk? But what had she said? And how long before she became the subject of speculation and gossip?

'I'm sorry, Claire,' Kit said, interrupting Claire's wayward thoughts. 'I didn't mean to upset you . . . '

'No, I'm all right,' Claire said, managing a faint smile. 'It's a bit complicated, that's all,' she added with a sigh.

'You don't have to explain. Not to me. Not to anyone,' Kit said softly. 'I thought you should know what Dani was saying.'

'Yes, thanks,' Claire said, appreciating the fact that Kit wasn't prying. She was silent for a long moment. 'I just never thought I'd ever see him again,' she said almost to herself, voicing the thought that had dropped into her mind.

'Are you talking about Daniel? Is he Dani's father?' Kit asked gently, effectively capturing Claire's attention.

'Yes, Daniel is her father,' Claire replied, finding it strange that each time she acknowledged this truth aloud, she felt a stab of both pain and pride.

'And you're still in love with him,' Kit stated matter-of-factly.

Claire's eyes flew to meet Kit's. There was no look of reproach, no censure in her tone, only understanding. 'Is it that obvious?' she asked.

'No. I just recognize the signs,' Kit said, sympathy and compassion in her smile. 'Ah, here come the children,' she continued, pointing to the small group, three of them dogs, walking up the path toward them. 'If you need someone to talk to, Claire, I'd be happy to listen. Just call,' Kit added, moments before the children joined them.

Claire deliberately pushed her troubled thoughts aside and for the next few minutes all that could be heard was the sound of barking dogs and children's excited chatter.

Dani, obviously forgetting that she hadn't been speaking to her mother, proceeded to tell Claire about the fun she'd had playing with Mark and the three dogs, Cleo and Piper, the two German shepherds, and Sooty, Mark's black Labrador puppy.

A little while later the men returned and Claire felt that quick tug of awareness as she glanced at Daniel.

That the two men had hit if off was obvious by the camaraderie and good-natured comments they exchanged.

For the next half hour the atmosphere was filled with warmth and laughter. Claire couldn't help noticing the tender glances Nathan and Kit exchanged. The way they smiled at each other left Claire with no doubt of the deep love they shared. And when Nathan stopped to drop a brief kiss on his wife's lips, a shiver of longing danced along Claire's spine.

'I'm sorry my mother wasn't here today, but tell Dorothy she'll drop by and see her soon,' Nathan said a little while later as they walked out to the car.

'Give your mother my love,' Kit told Claire. 'And call me,' she added, giving Claire a hug.

'Thanks,' Claire murmured as she climbed into the car.

Throughout the journey back to Peachville, Dani kept the conversation going, talking incessantly about Mark and the three dogs. When they arrived back at the house, Dorothy and Reginald were waiting eagerly to hear about the viewing. While the men talked, Claire began making dinner.

Glancing at her mother, Claire thought she looked rested and appeared to be in good spirits, no doubt glad to be home. Reginald looked happy, too, staying close to his wife, trying to anticipate her every need.

The upbeat celebratory mood lingered throughout dinner and Claire couldn't help smiling at the way Reginald hovered so solicitously over his wife, helping her in and out of her chair, patting pillows and continuously asking if she needed anything.

Claire noticed that her mother appeared to be watching Dani, who stayed near her father for the entire evening, even asking him to read her a story and put her to bed. Dorothy glanced at Claire on several occasions, obviously curious about Dani's behavior. But Claire smiled and made no comment, thinking there was time enough to tell her mother that Dani already knew the truth, feeling that there was little point making an announcement that would disrupt the evening.

It was later, as Claire lay in bed gazing at the ceiling, unable to sleep, that she let her thoughts drift over the day's events, to the moment when Daniel had mentioned marriage.

Pushing the sheet aside, she rose and slowly made her way downstairs to the kitchen.

Opening the door to the patio, she quietly walked out into the warm night air. The sky sparkled with the light of a million stars and Claire watched as a cloud hovered briefly near the moon before gliding eerily by.

What should she do? Should she marry Daniel? Silently she asked for the night's counsel, but neither the moon nor the stars gave her an answer. Daniel was right. Marriage would be a perfect solution — for him. Dani's relationship with her father had grown and blossomed in such a short time, but Claire couldn't quite banish the thought that perhaps Dani was simply a replacement for the child Daniel had lost so tragically.

While Claire knew Dani would be ecstatic to have a father of her own, especially her real father, she was fearful of putting her daughter at emotional risk. Dani's happiness and welfare had to be considered.

And what about love? Wasn't that an important consideration, too? That she loved Daniel totally and completely also entered into the equation. While her heart and soul might belong to Daniel, she had no idea whatsoever what his feelings for her might be.

Could she marry the man who was the father of her child, knowing he didn't return her love? Could she be truly happy in a one-sided relationship?

'Ahem.'

Claire gasped in surprise and spun around to see the subject of her thoughts standing in the patio doorway. His shirt was unbuttoned and in the glimmer of moonlight the muscles of his chest appeared to be carved in bronze, causing her pulse to skip a beat and her heart to shudder uncontrollably.

'Sorry. I didn't mean to frighten you,' Daniel said, taking a step toward her. 'I heard someone walking around down here and thought I'd check it out,' he explained.

Claire couldn't move or breathe. Her fingers itched to reach out and touch him, to trace the contours of his muscular chest and know again the heat, feel again the raging torrent of need he could so easily arouse within her.

'It's really hot out tonight,' Daniel continued, stopping a few inches from her.

Claire tried to swallow the lump of emotion clogging her throat, with no success.

'If I'm intruding, I'll go,' Daniel said.

Claire shook her head, still unable to speak, as all at once her thoughts swept her back in time to another night when the stars had shone equally as brightly, a night when he'd carried her from the water up onto the beach, a night when he'd taken her on the ultimate journey of discovery, stealing her heart on the way.

Daniel shifted his gaze to the night sky. He was silent for a long moment. 'The only thing missing is the ocean,' he said huskily, telling her clearly that he, too, had been visited by old memories.

Claire let her eyelids close, deliberately shutting out his image. But this action only served to heighten her awareness of him. She could feel his presence and knew that all she had to do was reach out and she'd be in his arms.

The earthy male scent that was his alone tickled her nostrils, invading her senses and stirring her soul. Her heart began to gather speed, like a runaway sled down a snow-covered mountain-side, sending pangs of yearning across her nerve endings, and bringing a soft sigh to her lips.

Kiss me! Kiss me! The words screamed insistently inside her head until she wondered if she was actually yelling them aloud.

'I think you want this almost as much as I do,' she heard Daniel say a split second before his mouth claimed hers.

And suddenly she was flying, soaring so high, it took her breath away. Up and up she flew, higher and higher as their tongues engaged in an age-old dance of desire, inciting a hunger, demanding a response she was only too eager to give.

She gloried in the white-hot flash of need that swept through her like lightning, a need she'd almost forgotten how to feel. She tasted the dark dusky flavor that was his desire as he crushed her against his muscular frame. And she felt the sizzling heat of his skin beneath her fingers almost as if he were on fire for her.

She groaned in protest when his mouth left hers to trace a moist trail down the curve of her neck and across her shoulder, pushing the cotton strap of her nightdress aside as he explored every aching, heated inch.

Her skin tingled as he made the return journey, stopping at the sensitive area below her ear for just a second, before nibbling at her lobe and flicking his tongue in and out in an erotic gesture that left her weak with longing.

Her heart began to beat at a frantic pace, and as she murmured his name over and over she felt him tremble against her. His mouth returned to claim hers in a kiss that rocked her to the core. Suddenly she was teetering helplessly on the edge of reason, her body and soul in total tune with the man who was kissing her as if he might never stop.

He couldn't seem to get enough. Soft, so incredibly soft. Hot, so unbelievably hot. Sexy, so damnably sexy. Daniel heard the blood pulsing in his veins, arousing a desire that tore through him with the speed of a rocket, driving him closer, ever closer to the edge.

She was everything he'd ever wanted, everything he'd ever needed, and the ache spreading like wildfire through him was almost more than he could endure.

Dragging his mouth from Claire's was one of the hardest things he'd ever had to do, but he knew if he didn't, he'd never be able to stop. Taking deep ragged breaths, he buried his face in the silky softness of her hair, savoring her sweetly seductive scent as he struggled to check the desire threatening to burn completely out of control.

'Claire. Claire.' Daniel murmured her name over and over, holding on, by the skin of his teeth, to the last remnants of his control.

Gradually he felt his heart begin to slow to a less punishing pace. He lifted his head to gaze into eyes the color of moonbeams, but when he glimpsed the look of raw desire mirrored in the depths of her eyes, he almost lost it all over again. 'We always were good together,' he whispered huskily.

At his words Claire froze. She felt as if she'd suddenly been plunged into an ice-cold pool and the desire that had been spiraling through her only seconds ago fizzled and died. Yes, the physical side of their relationship eight years ago had been both thrilling and wonderful, but she'd believed with all her heart then that he'd loved her as much as she'd loved him.

But there had been no words of love then and he was offering none now. And while sex without love might satisfy him, she knew for her it would never be enough. Because she wanted it all. She wanted his love. Always and forever.

The pain squeezing her heart brought the sting of tears to her eyes. Twisting out of his arms she ran toward the house and disappeared inside.

Daniel brought his fist down on the

railing and cursed under his breath. What had he done? A moment ago she'd been kissing him like there was no tomorrow. What the hell had happened? He dragged a trembling hand through his hair.

He'd all but convinced himself that she still had some feelings for him. The intensity of her response had startled, then amazed, then delighted him, driving him almost instantly to the edge. But now he was more confused than ever.

Why had she run away? Why did she seem determined to keep him at arm's length, especially when he'd had the impression earlier that they'd finally sorted out the mystery of the note he'd left for her in Paris?

Daniel rubbed the back of his neck as a feeling of frustration spread through him. She had to agree to marry him. No ifs, ands or buts about it. Yes, Dani needed a father as much as he needed his daughter, but that wasn't all. Claire was part of the equation, too . . . and if the truth be known, he realized with a jolt, she was in actuality the most important part.

From the moment he'd caught sight of her at the auction in Vancouver a week ago he'd found himself as captivated by her as he'd been eight years ago when he'd walked out of the water to find her trespassing on the beach.

She was the same, yet different, the intervening years having added a maturity as well as a feminine mystique that only served to enhance and enrich the woman who'd stolen his heart so long ago.

He'd admired her then for her straightforwardness, her openness and her strong sense of self, and he admired her now for the remarkable job she'd done raising their daughter, practically on her own.

But that job wasn't over, and while Daniel had missed the first seven years of his daughter's life, he was determined that he wasn't going to miss any more. But he wanted it all. He wanted the whole ball of wax. He wanted them to become a real family.

Family had always been important to him, and never more so than during those dark days after the accident that almost claimed his father's life. As the eldest son, Daniel had willingly accepted the responsibilities thrust on him during that painful time, rising to meet the challenge of keeping the family business running smoothly.

As a result he'd had to put his own life on hold, including his dream to reestablish and rebuild the side of the business that he loved best: restoration. He'd wanted to step out of the fast lane, to get away from the high-powered buying and selling of antiques and get back to the basics. He wanted to become more involved in the type of restoration work his grandfather had taught him.

It had been during those days in Italy when a plan for his future began to take shape in his mind, a plan needless to say he'd had to modify in the faint hope that Claire would agree to be a part of that future.

He hadn't said a word to Claire at the time, unsure whether or not she shared his feelings. Though he'd had high hopes on that score, he'd decided to wait until they met up again in Paris where he'd intended to surprise her with a proposal, hoping the romantic backdrop of the city would guarantee a positive response.

Fate, however, had stepped in to deal him an entirely different hand, a hand he'd been obliged to play for the past eight years, a hand he was more than ready to relinquish into the care of his younger brother, Paul, who for the past year had been eagerly waiting for the chance to prove to their father that he was as capable of running the business as either of them.

Daniel had quite recently spoken to his father in support of Paul's ambitions, taking the opportunity to mention his own feelings of discontent.

To his surprise his father had been openly receptive and quietly understanding, telling Daniel that he'd sensed his son's unhappiness and offering the advice that it was never too late to make changes.

Now, thanks to another twist of fate, Daniel had been given that all-too-elusive second chance. Those never-forgotten dreams were once again within his grasp, and he was damned if he was going to let them slip through his fingers a second time.

12

'Mother, what on earth are you doing in the kitchen?' Claire asked, when she came downstairs the next morning to find Dorothy in her housecoat, setting the table for breakfast.

Dorothy smiled. 'I know Dr. McGregor said to take things easy, but habits are hard to break, and that includes waking up early,' her mother said. 'I can't tell you how wonderful it is to be home,' she added with a sigh.

'There's nothing wrong with waking up early,' Claire said as she kissed her mother's cheek. 'But you're not supposed to do too much, remember?' Pulling a chair away from the table, she urged her mother to sit down.

'All right, you win,' Dorothy said, smiling at Claire. 'But I won't be coddled,' she said emphatically. She glanced quickly at the doorway then back at Claire. 'Reginald is driving me crazy,' she told Claire in a low voice. 'Is there any way you can persuade him to go to the auction with you today?'

'Mother!' Claire laughingly scolded, all the while thinking that she'd been looking for an excuse to stay home. After the tumultuous kiss she'd shared with Daniel the previous evening, Claire hadn't been looking forward to being alone with him.

Although she knew they'd be busy bidding on the various items he wanted to acquire, as well as keeping track of the selling price of other items at the auction, the thought of spending the day in close proximity with Daniel had kept her awake for most of the night.

'Please, darling,' Dorothy pleaded. 'Reginald chatted about the auction all day yesterday. I know he'd love to go and look around the house. I hear it's quite beautiful inside,' she went on.

'Yes, it is,' Claire replied.

'And to be quite honest, Claire,' her mother continued, glancing once more at the doorway, 'much as I love my husband, I do hate being treated like a porcelain doll.' She sighed. 'I know he means well, and in time he'll ease up, but how can I relax when he's hovering over me all the time?' she added in a slightly exasperated tone. 'You won't tell him I said that, will you?' she asked anxiously.

Claire laughed softly. 'Of course not, Mother,' she replied.

'Oh, good morning, Daniel,' Dorothy said brightly.

'Good morning,' Daniel replied as he entered the kitchen. 'How are you this morning? No aftereffects from the homecoming celebration last night?' he asked teasingly as he crossed to the fridge.

'None at all,' Dorothy answered with a smile.

Claire felt her heart flutter inside her breast in reaction to the sound of Daniel's deep voice. She kept her back to him, deliberately giving all her attention to filling the coffee carafe with water. But her traitorous body couldn't ignore the presence of the man she loved, and a tingling awareness shimmied through her, creating a trail of erotic sensations.

'What about you, Claire? Did you sleep well?' Daniel asked, moving to stand next to her, almost, but not quite, touching her.

Desire, strong and potent, vibrated through her, and it took every ounce of Claire's self-control not to move closer. Her whole body began to quiver as the clean male scent of his after-shave enveloped her, assailing her senses and arousing needs she'd just as soon forget. It wasn't fair that he should have such a devastating effect on her, she thought, as she clung with quiet desperation to a control that was teetering dangerously on the edge.

'I slept very well, thank you,' she lied. Reaching for the coffee canister, she proceeded to measure coffee into the filter.

'Me, too,' he said. 'What time are we

leaving for the auction this morning?' he asked evenly.

'Actually, I was just saying that I think Reginald should go with you today,' Claire replied, switching on the machine.

'Is my name being taken in vain? Or am I being volunteered for something?' Reginald asked teasingly as he joined them in the kitchen.

Dorothy smiled at her husband as he bent to kiss her forehead. 'Claire wondered if you'd like to go to the auction with Daniel today, dear.'

Reginald glanced at Claire. 'Well, I must admit I'd be very interested in seeing some of the pieces you and Daniel were talking about yesterday,' he commented. 'But it's your first day home, my dear — '

'I'll be fine, Reginald,' Dorothy quickly cut in, flashing her husband a reassuring smile. 'Besides, Claire and Dani will be here to keep me company,' she went on.

'You should go, Reg.' Claire added

her support. 'There were a few paintings throughout the house that are worth taking a look at,' she added, knowing her stepfather had a soft spot for artwork.

'Claire's right,' Daniel said. 'And I wouldn't mind soliciting your valuable opinion on a couple of items,' he went on.

'Well, if it's all right with you, my dear,' Reginald said, touching his wife's shoulder.

When the men departed a short time later, Claire was surprised at the stab of disappointment she felt as she watched them drive away. After a hurried breakfast, Dani, too, made a quick exit, announcing that she was going next door to play with Taylor.

'Have you spoken to Dani about her father yet?' Dorothy asked once they'd finished clearing away the breakfast dishes and moved to the living room to linger over a fresh cup of coffee.

'Yes,' Claire said. 'She knows Daniel's her father.'

'How did she take it?' Dorothy asked as she settled herself in the rocker-recliner in front of the bay window.

Claire sank into the easy chair opposite and sighed, remembering all too clearly how Dani had learned the news. 'She was rather upset,' Claire said. 'But that was my fault. I didn't handle it well,' she confessed. 'Daniel and I were arguing and Dani overheard me saying that I wasn't going to tell her he was her father.'

'Oh, Claire. How awful for Dani . . . and for you, too,' her mother commiserated.

'She's still angry with me,' Claire said. 'That's why she's doing her best to avoid me. I want to explain things to her, but she's not ready to listen yet.'

'She's quite taken with Daniel.' Dorothy voiced the observation. 'That should help,' she added. 'But what about you? How are you coping with all of this? Has Daniel told you what he plans to do? What are his rights, anyway?'

Claire was silent for a long moment. 'Daniel thinks we should get married,' she said at last.

'Married?' her mother repeated, throwing Claire a startled glance. 'But that's wonderful,' she went on excitedly. 'Isn't it?' she added, frowning in puzzlement at Claire.

Claire shook her head. 'Not when the only reason he's suggesting marriage is because it will allow him unlimited access to his daughter,' she said, trying with difficulty to keep the ache in her heart out of her voice.

'Oh, I see,' Dorothy said softly. 'You're still in love with him, aren't you?'

Claire laughed aloud, but there was no humor in the sound. 'What is this? Am I wearing a placard around my neck with the words I Love Daniel Hunter written on it?' she asked ruefully, recalling how Kit had made a similar observation.

Dorothy's smile was sad. 'You don't need a placard, darling. I can see it in your eyes,' her mother said.

'Then I'd better buy myself a pair of dark glasses,' Claire said, attempting to keep the tone light.

Suddenly her composure crumbled and she covered her face with her hands. 'What am I going to do?' she asked, her voice quivering with emotion, tears spilling down her face.

'Darling, don't cry,' her mother gently urged. 'You'll do what you feel is best. You always have. But let me offer you a word of advice,' she went on. 'If you are still in love with Daniel, then maybe half a loaf of bread would be better than no loaf.'

Claire made no comment. Numerous times during the long lonely night she'd had the exact same thought.

Throughout the morning, several neighbors and friends dropped in while others called to ask about Dorothy's progress. Claire fielded some calls and tried to ensure that no one stayed too long or tired her mother too much.

It was after lunch, when Dorothy

returned to her room for a nap, that Claire found herself alone with Dani. She'd expected Dani to make excuses and return next door to play, but she seemed in no hurry to leave.

'Dani, I think it's time we had a talk,' Claire said as she finished putting the dishes in the dishwasher.

'What about?' Dani asked, the hint of a challenge in her voice.

Claire pulled out the chair next to Dani and sat facing her. 'I know you're angry at me right now, and you have every right to be. I should have told you about Daniel from the start,' she acknowledged. 'But the night he flew your grandfather and me back from Vancouver all I could think of was Grandma and whether she was going to be all right. You and your grandmother had been through a lot that night, and I didn't think the time to tell you was right then. You'd had enough to deal with.' She ground to a halt, hoping Dani would respond. But she kept her head bent, her eyes down.

'Daniel wanted me to tell you but I kept putting it off. He was right, and I'm sorry I didn't tell you sooner. Do you think you can forgive me?' Claire asked, her voice trembling just a little.

Claire watched as Dani slowly lifted her head. Gray eyes, so like her father's, glistened with unshed tears. 'You should have told me,' Dani said in a tiny voice.

'I know, darling. I'm sorry,' Claire replied. 'Aw . . . sweetheart. Please don't cry,' she went on, feeling tears gathering in her own eyes. Reaching out, she gently pulled her daughter's unresisting body off the chair and into her arms.

Claire hugged Dani until she stopped crying. Dani sniffed loudly as she pulled away to gaze up at her mother. 'I like Daniel,' Dani said. 'I like him a lot,' she added.

At her daughter's words, a pain sliced through her heart, but Claire ignored it. 'I'm glad,' she said, managing a watery smile.

'He's big and strong and he's fun to be with,' Dani went on, as if she were trying to convince Claire. 'He teached me how to dive and he says I'm the best pupil he's ever had,' she rushed on. 'And he's promised that he will take me up in his plane one day.' She paused, but only for a moment. 'He's exactly what I've always dreamed a daddy would be like . . . what my daddy would be like,' Dani went on, her eyes sparkling, her smile almost as bright as the sun outside.

Claire blinked away fresh tears as she kept her own smile in place. 'He loves you very much,' Claire said, knowing she was speaking the truth, and knowing, too, after what Dani had just said, that the decision hanging over her, the decision she had to make about their future, would be all the harder to make.

'What's going to happen now?' Dani wanted to know. 'I know Daniel lives far away, 'cause he told me. If he goes away, will he still be my daddy?'

Claire swallowed the lump of emotion clogging her throat. 'He'll always be your daddy,' Claire said. 'And I know he'll want to see you and spend as much time as he possibly can with you,' she added. 'There are a few things he and I have to figure out about that,' she continued, unwilling to say more, but Dani nodded, seemingly content at the moment with Claire's answer.

For the remainder of the day Dani played in and around the house. As the afternoon wore on Claire found herself watching and listening for the men to return. It seemed strange somehow that during the past week she'd grown accustomed to having Daniel around, accustomed to seeing him sitting across the table from her at mealtimes. She even confessed to herself that she'd looked forward to those moments when he'd thrown her a fleeting smile or made a teasing comment.

He'd told her he wanted an answer before he left for Boston, and indeed there seemed little point in prolonging matters, but she was no nearer making a decision about the future than she'd been when he'd put forth his suggestion of what he'd deemed the 'perfect solution.'

When Reg and Daniel returned from the auction, Dani rushed to greet her father, squealing in delight when he lifted her high in the air. Silently Claire acknowledged the leap her heart took at the sight of him, wishing he would look at her the way he was looking at Dani.

Conversation during dinner centered around the auction and the pieces they'd bid on successfully, as well as the items that had sold for a lower or higher price. But after dinner Reginald and Daniel withdrew to Reginald's office saying they wanted to consult further about the next day's auction, leaving Claire to wonder if Daniel had forgotten all about the ultimatum he'd handed her.

On Sunday morning Daniel and Reginald headed to the auction right after breakfast, leaving Claire to spend the day trying to convince herself that if she accepted Daniel's proposal, somehow, some way, she would make him fall in love with her.

She knew she was only fooling herself, and as the afternoon dragged on a feeling of despair settled over her.

For the second time in as many days, Claire watched and waited for the men to return. When they appeared late in the afternoon, Claire couldn't help feeling as she watched Daniel and Reginald exchange glances, that something unusual had happened at the auction, something neither man was prepared to discuss.

During dinner Claire tried unsuccessfully to coax Reginald into revealing the secret both men seemed intent on keeping. But each time Reginald appeared on the verge of divulging some small piece of information, Daniel managed to steer the conversation to another topic, leaving Claire puzzled and frustrated.

It was while Claire, with Dani's help,

was putting the dishes in the dish-washer that the telephone rang.

'Daniel, it's your father,' Reginald said a few minutes later. 'He wants to talk to you.'

'Would you mind if I took the call in your office?' Daniel asked as he rose from the dinner table.

'By all means,' Reginald said.

Fifteen minutes later Daniel reap-peared and Claire watched as his glance went first to his daughter then to her. 'Claire, we need to talk,' he said. 'How about we take a stroll along the banks of the stream?' he suggested.

'Can I come, too?' Dani asked, jumping up from the floor where she'd been happily coloring with her crayons.

'Not this time, poppet,' Daniel said, softening his words with a smile. 'Your mother and I have something important to discuss.'

'But I — ' Dani started to protest.

'How about a game of cards with your grandfather and me?' Dorothy quickly intervened.

Dani looked first at Daniel then at Claire. 'Okay,' she relented. 'Can we play Happy Families?' she asked.

'Sure,' Dorothy replied. 'Run upstairs and get the cards,' she said, and Dani scurried off.

'Shall we?' Daniel said, and Claire had little choice but to agree.

The path through the backyard led to a tiny stream that ran parallel to the road at the front of the house. Outside, the evening air was starting to cool as the sun made its nightly descent in the west.

Claire tucked her hands in the pockets of her skirt to hide her nervousness, feeling like a teenager on her first date, unsure what to say or how to act. As they took the well-trodden route along the banks of the stream, a shiver of apprehension skipped down her spine and she wished she'd grabbed her lightweight sweater to throw over the scoop-necked turquoise top she wore.

'My father wanted to know what was

keeping me here,' Daniel said, breaking the silence at last. 'He wants me back in Boston. Said it was time I got back to taking care of the business.'

'Does he know about Dani?' Claire asked, lengthening her stride a little to match his.

'No, I haven't told my family anything' came the reply.

'I see,' Claire said, not seeing at all, and wondering at his reason for keeping his family in the dark.

'I thought I'd wait until you gave me your answer,' he said, slowing to a halt. They'd reached the small covered miniature wooden bridge that was a favorite spot for courting couples, but tonight there was no one around, only the birds chattering in the trees nearby and the sound of the water trickling over the stones beneath the bridge.

Daniel turned to face her and Claire was surprised to see the look of anxiety that flashed in the depths of his gray eyes, before it was gone like a bird on the wing.

'What is your answer, Claire?' he asked. 'Will you marry me?'

Claire drew a shaky breath. Inside she was slowly dying. How often had she dreamed of Daniel saying those words to her? Her heart was urging her to say yes, but her head was telling her that she could never be completely happy in a marriage as one-sided as theirs would surely be. 'I'm sorry,' she said at last. 'I just don't think it would work. My answer has to be no.'

Daniel felt as if he'd suddenly been punched in the stomach. Had she really said no?

Dazed and reeling from the shock, he drew a ragged breath. 'Why?' he asked huskily. 'Are you worried about Dani? Don't you think she'd be happy if we got married?'

'She'd be thrilled,' Claire said, 'but you don't understand — '

'You can say that again,' Daniel cut in, anger overriding every other emotion. 'If we got married, we'd be a real family. Isn't that what every kid wants, what every kid deserves?' he added, fighting to keep the desperation he was feeling from his voice.

'Yes,' Claire replied, keeping her tone even. 'But much as I want Dani to be happy, it isn't just Dani's happiness that's at stake here,' she continued, trying with difficulty to hold on to her temper. She hadn't expected his anger, hadn't anticipated this volatile reaction at all.

All at once Daniel grasped her upper arms, pulling her toward him until their bodies were almost touching, his mouth barely inches from hers. 'We could make it work, Claire. I know we could,' he said huskily, his breath fanning her face, sending a delicious tremor racing through her.

With her knees threatening to buckle under her, she fought the urge to melt against him. 'It isn't enough, Daniel. It just isn't enough,' she repeated, her voice vibrating with pain.

'What do you mean, it isn't enough?' Daniel demanded, his eyes darkening to a deep silver, his jaw tense with anger.

Claire sighed. 'What I'm trying to say is that being good in bed together isn't enough,' she said in a choked voice. 'I want to know that the man I'm marrying loves me as much as I love him. A relationship based on lust is doomed to fail. I want more. I want it all. But you don't love me, Daniel. That's why I can't marry you,' she concluded, as the tears she'd been fighting to hold in check spilled down her cheeks.

She tried to wrench free of his grasp, wanting to run away, wanting to be alone. She'd just finished baring her soul to him. She'd just told him she loved him and she didn't want to see the look of pity she was sure she would see in his eyes.

'Don't love you! How can you say I don't love you?' Daniel charged. 'Damn it, Claire, you're the only woman I've ever loved,' he told her with a fierceness that shocked her.

Her heartbeat accelerated, her eyes flew to meet his, needing confirmation that the words he'd uttered were true.

'But what about Kelly?' The question came from that dark corner of her heart that refused to believe. 'She was your wife. You must have loved her,' Claire said, trying desperately to calm her racing pulse.

Daniel closed his eyes for a moment and inhaled deeply. 'What I felt for Kelly wasn't love,' he confessed, his expression bleak now. 'I felt sorry for her, that's all, and for a while I convinced myself it was love. By the time I realized I'd been fooling myself, that I'd never stopped loving you, it was too late,' he went on.

'You don't marry someone you feel sorry for,' Claire said, still unconvinced.

'We were friends,' he said. 'Our fathers were business associates, and we saw a good deal of each other. When Kelly's father died in that accident, she was devastated. She had no one to turn to, no one to lean on. And so she turned to me.' He sighed, an abundance of emotion in the sound.

'I kept expecting to hear from you,' he went on. 'But when you didn't call and no letter arrived I had to push the memory of our time together to the back of my mind, locking it away forever. It was just too painful to think about. I kept telling myself that I'd been wrong about you, that what we'd had together was nothing more than a holiday romance.

'Kelly was always there. I suppose you could say we needed each other.' There was pain and sadness in his voice now. Daniel closed his eyes, giving Claire the impression he was looking back in time. 'I proposed because it seemed the right thing to do, and almost before I could say Jack Robinson, the wedding plans were underway. Once the train had pulled out of the station there didn't seem to be any way to stop it.

'And after a while I just couldn't bring myself to hurt Kelly,' he added. 'Not when she seemed so happy. But it wasn't long before we both realized we'd made a mistake. By then Kelly was pregnant.' He stopped and took a steadying breath. 'I think we felt that the baby might bring us closer together, fill in the gaps in our relationship. And he did. At least for a short time. Kevin's death put an end to what little feelings we had left for each other,' he concluded sadly.

'It must have been difficult for you both,' Claire said, her heart aching for him, hearing the pain echoing through him.

'We should never have gotten married,' he said. 'I should never have gone through with it, because somewhere deep inside I knew I'd never stopped loving you.'

Claire felt the tears sting her eyes, scarcely able to believe what he'd said. 'But you never told me,' she accused softly. 'You never said a word. And when you didn't show up in Paris, I thought you'd had a change of heart.'

Daniel released his hold on her arms and brought his hands up to gently cradle her face. 'You're right. I should have told you how I felt,' he said, his eyes gazing tenderly into hers. He kissed her forehead, then her eyelids, next her cheek, stopping just short of her lips. 'I'd planned it all out, you see,' he told her huskily. 'A romantic evening in one of the most romantic cities. After dining and dancing at one of my favorite restaurants, I was going to take you on a moonlight stroll along the banks of the Seine. There, under the stars, I'd planned to tell you that I loved you.'

Claire sighed, thinking how wonderful it would have been, how wonderful it should have been.

'I know this isn't Paris,' she began shyly. 'And I know the little stream behind us doesn't look at all like the Seine, but maybe we could pretend just for a minute.'

A smile curved at the corner of Daniel's mouth. He held her away from him and gazed intently into her eyes. 'Claire, I love you with all my heart,' he said with a sincerity that touched her soul.

'And I love you,' Claire replied a second before his lips claimed hers.

The kiss was everything she'd ever dreamed of and more. She could almost taste the love and the need, matching them easily with her own. This was what she had longed for, this was what she was born for. Daniel was her soul mate, the only man she would ever love.

As their bodies strove to be closer, as their mouths expressed their hunger for each other, Claire knew with a deep certainty the dream she'd been secretly harboring, the dream she'd kept in her heart for so long, had suddenly come true.

Daniel broke the kiss, hugging Claire tightly until the storm raging through them both began to subside. 'I think this time I'd better get it right,' he said, and Claire heard the hint of humor in his voice.

'Get what right?' she asked, still breathless from the kiss.

'Will you marry me?' Daniel asked, his voice throbbing with emotion.

Tears stung her eyes and her heart seemed to do a little dance of joy as she held his gaze. 'Yes!' She shouted the word at the top of her voice, startling the birds, causing them to abandon the treetops in a flutter of panic.

Daniel's kiss this time was brief but utterly devastating, leaving her clinging to him weakly, her heart thundering inside her chest to keep time with his.

'I knew I should have bought a ring,' he said, laughter in his voice now. 'But with the auction going on, I just didn't have time,' he went on. 'But I did buy you something at the auction I thought you might like,' he added, a twinkle of amusement in his eyes.

Her heart melted. 'You bought me something at the auction?' she said, deeply touched by the fact that he'd obviously been thinking about her. 'Is that what you and Reginald were being so secretive about?' she asked.

Daniel laughed, and the deep rich

sound sent her blood humming through her veins.

'Reginald was a bit surprised, I must admit,' he said. 'Does he know about you and me and Dani?'

'Never mind about that,' Claire said. 'What did you buy me?' she asked growing more curious by the minute. 'Tell me!' she demanded.

Daniel smiled. 'Everything depended on whether or not you accepted my proposal, of course,' he told her, obviously enjoying teasing her.

'I just did,' Claire reminded him.

'Yes, my darling, I know,' Daniel said, kissing her nose. 'That's what I was counting on. Because if we are going to be married, then we'll need a place to live, a home of our own,' he said.

'A home of our own?' Claire repeated, still puzzled. 'Are you trying to tell me you've bought a house?' she asked incredulously.

'Not just any house — Braeside estate,' Daniel said, his eyes twinkling. 'Now that we're finally going to be a family, it would be the perfect home for us. And maybe sometime in the near future, we could add a brother or sister for Dani. What do you think?'

Claire thought her heart would burst. 'Oh, Daniel, it's absolutely perfect. No, *perfect* doesn't even begin to describe it,' she said as she wrapped her arms around him and lifted her mouth to meet his. Their love had stood the test of time. There would be no more misunderstandings, no more mistakes. This time was forever.

THE END

We do hope that you have enjoyed reading this large print book.

Did you know that all of our titles are available for purchase?

We publish a wide range of high quality large print books including:
Romances, Mysteries, Classics
General Fiction
Non Fiction and Westerns

Special interest titles available in large print are:
The Little Oxford Dictionary
Music Book, Song Book
Hymn Book, Service Book

Also available from us courtesy of Oxford University Press:
Young Readers' Dictionary
(large print edition)
Young Readers' Thesaurus
(large print edition)

For further information or a free brochure, please contact us at:
Ulverscroft Large Print Books Ltd.,
The Green, Bradgate Road, Anstey,
Leicester, LE7 7FU, England.
Tel: (00 44) **0116 236 4325**
Fax: (00 44) **0116 234 0205**

EARL GRESHAM'S BRIDE

Angela Drake

When heiress Kate Roscoe compromises herself through an innocent mistake, widower, Earl Gresham steps in with an offer of marriage to save her reputation. She is soon deeply in love with him, but is beset by the problems of overseeing his grand household. The housekeeper is dishonest and the nanny of the earl's two children is heartless and lazy. But a far greater threat comes from his former mistress who will go to any lengths to destroy Kate's marriage.

FINDING ANNABEL

Paula Williams

Annabel had disappeared after going to meet the woman who, she'd just discovered, was her natural mother . . . However, when her sister Jo travels to Somerset to try and find her, she must follow a trail of lies and deceit. The events of the past and the present have become dangerously entangled. And she discovers, to her cost, that for some people in the tiny village of Neston Parva, old loyalties remain fierce and strangers are not welcome . . .

IT WAS ALWAYS YOU

Miranda Barnes

Anna Fenwick is very fond of Matthew, a hard-working young man from her Northumberland village. She has known him all her life, although, sadly, it seems that he is not interested in her. Then Anna embarks on a whirlwind romance with Don, a visiting Canadian and goes to Calgary with him. Life is wonderful for a time. However, her heart is still in Northumberland — but when she returns to seek Matthew, will she eventually find him?

IN HER SHOES

Anne Holman

Inspector Mallison was reluctant to arrest the murdered man's son, although the incriminating evidence was overwhelming: he'd been alone with his father immediately prior to the murder and there'd been a bitter quarrel; Goldstein was killed trying to alter his will — unfavourably for his son; the weapon, a desk paperweight bore the son's fingerprints, and his father had withdrawn financial support for a new West End play in which his son was to star. Yet still Mallinson wasn't convinced . . .